THE FIFTH PLANE

A Tangled Web

Vol 11.

A Novel

By

Val Walker

E BOOK: 978-1-968165-48-2

PAPERBACK: 978-1-968165-49-9

HARDBACK: 978-1-968165-50-5

Published by **American Book Publisher**: 2025

www. americanbookpublisher.com

Dedication

TO EVERYDAY HEROES

AND THE FLIGHT CREWS OF 9/11

Acknowledgment

To CORY. Thank you for being the kind, wise and amazing man and son you are. You are my unsung hero.

STEPHEN TRYON - AKA/PES. You always had my '6 as a FAM, friend and a crucial source of security information during the days I was flying following 9/11. My technical advisor before, during and after writing The 5th Plane. My BFF friend for life.

USAF Lt. COLONEL AHMED RAGHEB A wise and patient friend. Fellow Red Star pilot, artist, poet and USAF Lt. Colonel. Thank you for your time and patience in helping me understand. Gone too soon. You are missed by all.

WESTERN and DELTA AIRLINES. Thank you for giving me the profession of my dreams, the experiences of a lifetime and the unique and wonderful crews to share them with.

MEMOIR WRITERS GROUP.

BILL and JERRI MELLAS, LAURA and ELLEN. My extended family who chose me for theirs. Thank you for your unwavering love and support during the writing of The 5th Plane.

To my dad CLINT WALKER who was and still is an inspiration and guiding light to millions of people worldwide. His legacy lives on through all of us whose lives he touched.

About the Author

DAL Captain Valerie Walker was flying Delta Boeing 767s and 757s out of Boston, La Guardia and New York JFK all month during September of 2001. September 11th was her day off. On September 14th a handful of airliners were permitted to fly again for the first time since 9/11 had shut down the skies over America. New York's River visual approach took Captain Walker's flight between the illuminated beauty of the Statue of Liberty on her Left and the smoldering ruins of the twin Towers on her co-pilot's right. The smell of death permeated the cockpit, breaking their hearts and strengthening their resolve." Never again. Not on our watch."

Val has written over 156 articles as managing editor, Art Director and flight test pilot for Plane & Pilot, Air Racing and Air Progress magazines, as well as Rotor & Wing and ALPA magazines. A first-degree Black Belt in Kenpo Karate, and student of Kendo, Wing Chun, Jiu-Jitsu and Krav Maga, she teaches defense for flight Crews and owns

Raptor Tactical Martial Arts. Her Police Aerial Patrol Helicopter pilot wings and badge were displayed in the Smithsonian Museum as the first female police aerial patrol helicopter pilot. Val's Western and Delta Airline Pilot uniforms were displayed in the 99's Museum and other museums across the country as one of the first six female airline pilots hired in the US. Captain Walker was hired by Western Airlines on March 8th 1976 in their first class with a female airline pilot in it.

Thousands of airline pilots volunteered when the Federal Flight Deck Officer program was developed for US airline pilots to train to fight and carry firearms in the cockpit after 9/11. Captain Walker was chosen in the first official class of 40 airline pilots nationwide to train at the Federal Law Enforcement Training Center (FLETC) and be deputized to defend the cockpit and her aircraft against terrorists. You can find many articles and videos about her online. People Magazine, ALPA magazine, The LA Times and other publications have followed her throughout her career.

She is a member of the National Aviation and Space Writers Association, the Aviation Writers Club, The 99's, The Whirley Girls and a charter founding member of ISA+21. Her pilot Certificates include Flight Engineer - commercial single and multi-engine - helicopter, rotorcraft- CFI – Instrument and seaplane ratings. Valerie has Airline Transport ratings on the DC-3/ B737/B727/B757/B767.

Captain Walker is a member of the Red Star Pilots Association and owns and flies her Chinese military Nanchang CJ-6, donating aerobatic rides for charities.

Val lives happily in Utah and enjoys hiking with her Akita Ashi, skiing, reading, writing, painting, working with raptors at Hawk Watch, and riding horses and motorcycles with her friends. She plays classical guitar, kayaks and enjoys friends, family, small miracles, and each new adventure life has to offer. Of the two wolves fighting inside us, she chooses to feed the good wolf.

Table of Contents

The Last Steps Before the Storm

The last embers of sunlight bled into the horizon as Atta stood alone in the quiet of their makeshift sanctuary. The world outside was restless, alive with the usual hum of distant planes and everyday distractions, but inside, the silence was deafening. He allowed himself one moment of reflection, letting the weight of his plans settle over him.

"We are ready," he muttered to himself, his voice barely a whisper, as though saying it aloud might give it too much power. The Brigades of Belief were gathering, and the final pieces were falling into place.

Marwan's voice broke through the stillness, laced with a tinge of doubt. "But what if they're not prepared? What if the plan falls apart?"

Atta turned sharply, his gaze hard and unwavering. "Then we adjust. But nothing will stop us. It must begin."

Outside, the world seemed to hold its breath. The thunder in the distance felt like the drumroll before the storm. As the sky darkened further, Atta's mind shifted, calculating the next steps. They were no longer mere men; soon, they would become the hands of destiny.

Tomorrow, everything would change.

Chapter Twenty-One
The Brigades of Belief

April. 2, 2001 / 07:50 am EST / Miami International Airport

"We will get you. We will humiliate you. We will never stop following you."

- **Abdul Aziz al-Omari, "Al-Qaeda terrorist" deceased**

"Cherokee Five-five-four Hotel Alpha do - you - read – Miami – Ground - Control?" The exasperated controller repeated it for the fourth time. The little low-wing Piper Cherokee Warrior sat motionless on a taxiway, blocking a United 767 and an assortment of Air Jamaica and Value Jet DC-9s. Hot muggy air and thunderheads working themselves up into an approaching line of thunderstorms were not improving anyone's disposition.

"Miami Ground this is United 1325 heavy." a professional voice responded.

"Go ahead United." the controller barked, anxious to get back to the unresponsive Cherokee Warrior.

"We've been sitting behind this Cherokee for the last twenty minutes." the voice drawled.

"I'm aware of that." the controller snapped "Stand by!"

"Sorry ground, but I think you need to hear this." the United pilot continued. "Two guys just got out of that aircraft about ten minutes ago. They walked down the taxiway and across runways eight right and nine left. Then they climbed over the fence. Cherokee 554 Hotel Alpha appears to be empty".

"What?"

"He said that the two yay-hoos in that aluminum road block just bailed out, broke about twenty FAA regulations and sauntered down your taxiway, across two runways, over the fence and over the river and through the woods to grandma's house for all we know." Value Jet chimed in. "Get somebody to tow that thing off the taxiway so we can get out of here before the storm hits!"

"Stand by everyone!" the controller directed, whipping his binoculars up and muttering "I don't believe this!" It only took him a minute to determine that the Cherokee was indeed empty and the engine was not running.

"Chuck!" the controller shouted at his subordinate "Grab a land line and have a tug tow that airplane out of there. Then get the Feds to find out who it belongs to and who those idiots were that left it on my taxiway."

"Consider it done boss." the young trainee responded. His freckles stood out in the excitement of being entrusted with a real challenge.

"All right people. Listen up." the controller broadcast over the ground frequency. "We're getting you all out of here before that front hits." he promised. "Here's what we're going to do…"

The approaching cumulonimbus were spattering the leaves and marshy ground around them in wet ripe bursts. Atta and Al-Shehhi scrambled over the chicken wire fence on the North side of Miami International Airport.

"Marwan!" Atta directed. "Get off the fence and hurry up. It's beginning to rain!"

Marwan Al-Shehhi redoubled his efforts to free his pant leg from the strand of barbed wire. "I am coming Mohamed!" he replied from his awkward perch. Atta turned and strode off through the tall grass. The truculent wire finally ripped through the cloth, dropping Marwan in an undignified heap on the other side. He picked himself up and started after his leader in a swarm of disturbed grasshoppers. "Wait Mohamed." he entreated. "I am coming!"

Atta was the smaller man, but the needs of his body seemed of no importance to him. He wore the numerous self-inflicted cuts from the barbed wire as if they were the bloodied scourge wounds of a penitent priest. Atta rarely ate these days. *He enjoys the ways of the martyr.* Marwan thought as he watched Atta's rigid form plodding through the weeds in front of him. *He likes pain. It makes him feel alive.*

Wind gusts whipped around them as they slogged on through the mud toward the airport perimeter road. Marwan used the situation to distract himself from wondering about his leaders' personality disorders. *At least the rain cools the air and keeps the mosquitoes down.* he thought, raising his face to the darkening sky.

This much water all the time was uncomfortable for the two men from the desert. But then, so was everything else about this place. It was a constant source of stress. As was their necessary state of daily paranoia.

"Allah be praised." Marwan murmured as a local highway and Seven-Eleven came into view. Before they could get there Atta dropped to his knees facing Mecca and began the third set of prayers for the day. Marwan knelt in the wet weeds beside him. The mud would have to do in place of traditional prayer rugs. Once finished, the men got up and brushed themselves off. A delayed jet roared overhead. The disheveled pair sloshed out of the rain and into the welcoming confines of the convenience store. They bought themselves cherry and grape Slushies.

Atta called a cab. They went outside to wait for it under the eaves. A little heat and rain were preferable to freezing in the air-conditioned store.

"I had hoped for a better flight today." Atta commented, squatting against the wall and throwing his barely touched drink aside. The two men had been working on their private pilot, commercial, multi-engine and instrument pilot licenses over the last year. This extreme effort would seem strange to anyone but the perfection driven Atta, considering the fact they intended to die within the next few months. It also provided an effective cover for them to continue to operate in America on their student Visas.

"The airplane was bad. Bad maintenance. It quit on us." Atta continued. "Everything in this Godless place is bad." he ruminated sourly. Marwan nodded in sympathetic agreement. He silently worried that they had left the airplane where they would be held accountable for it.

Atta's decision to fly into the busy Miami Dade International Airport had been his way of flaunting their attainment under the noses of the Americans. He had forgotten to apply carburetor heat in the humid conditions and flooded the little aircraft's engine in his attempts to restart it. Atta and Marwan had an unspoken agreement. The fault was attributable to a flight school maintenance problem with the Piper Cherokee Warrior. Not operator error.

"Here!" Atta stood and waved a rusty yellow and black checkered cab over. The Jamaican driver pulled up and got out, opening the door for the men. He gave them an inquiring sneer as he surveyed their bloodied and muddied condition.

"You da two 'fellas who call me to take you two "hunnret miles to Venice mon?" he asked Atta. "Dat gonna' cost you big" he stated, doubting they could pay. Atta pulled out a thick roll of twenty-dollar bills and jabbed it at the driver as he slid into the back seat.

The dreadlocked Jamaican's eyes widened as he took the money and thumbed through it, calculating a sixty-dollar tip. The roll added up to four hundred dollars.

Atta slammed the door and Marwan slid in the other side. "Drive." Atta demanded, giving the cabbie an irritated glance.

"O.K. mon. No problem." he said, pocketing the money. He wondered if they were drug dealers. The cab pulled out onto the Interstate and headed West. *Who knows?* he thought. *In dis job you see every'ting and you learn to mind yo own business.* As far as he was concerned the less contact he had with the strange cold-eyed man in his back seat the better.

The three-hour cab ride to the West Coast of Florida gave Atta time to review their plans. When he spoke to Marwan he spoke in Dari. The driver continued ignoring them and turned up the volume on his Reggae station. His dread locks bobbed in time with Jimmy Cliff's taunting anti-establishment lyrics. "Police Officer, are you a worrier?"

"Shouldn't we not stop and contact the flight school to tell them where we left the airplane?" Marwan asked nervously.

"No." Atta responded. "That is their problem because it is their bad airplane. I have more important worries." he stated matter-of-factly. The event was only a few months away now and the "Brigades of Belief" (as their supplier, Sheik Omar called them) were arriving. These men had been trained in hand-to-hand combat in the Al Qaeda camps. Their only tasks were to physically overpower passengers and flight crews and keep them away from the cockpit, or to fly the civilian airliners into their assigned targets in unison on the day of the event. The Al Qaeda pilots were the leaders. The new men would be the muscle. They would be entering the "Jihad on America" through the cool jetways and concrete parking structures of the nation. Mostly in pairs. There would be no weak moments. No going back now. Each partner was also an Al Qaeda watchdog, making sure the other showed no signs of backing out. Atta was responsible for managing them when they arrived.

"We must leave Venice and start searching for apartments near Fort

Lauderdale." He said. "We will set up our next base of operations there." The cab sliced along the straight corridor that I-75 cut through the everglades. Marwan glanced out at the swampy expanses of Alligator Alley, quietly anticipating living in another city.

"Nine of our brothers will be arriving during the next two months." Atta continued. "It is our task to receive and guide them until the holy event." Atta turned to Marwan as he spoke, but he looked through him. Not at him. His attention was on putting events into play and reviewing every detail in his mind. Marwan was just a sounding board. Atta scowled as he addressed an unpleasant inevitability.

"We will have to take Jarrah with us." Atta uttered Ziad Jarrah's name as if it tasted bad. "If he can be found away from that woman that he vacations with." Atta added in disgust. He was referring to Jarrah's beautiful Westernized wife, Aysel.

Ziad lied to Aysel about his activities in America. His long periods of silence were always followed by proclamations of undying love to her. As far she knew, he was training to become a real airline pilot and they would have a wonderful life together. Atta saw Aysel as a threat and an affront to Islam itself. He saw Jarrah as weak and a potential traitor.

Marwan watched the anger rise and color drain from Atta's face. He knew that Atta was remembering Bin Laden ordering him to stop trying to dominate Jarrah on this issue. The Al Qaeda poster boy had made it clear that they could not afford to lose another pilot. Jarrah was threatening to leave because of Atta's attempts to bully him. This challenge to Atta's absolute authority enraged and humiliated him. He felt disrespected and emasculated. The controlled thoughts of the little terrorist leader turned to Aysel and her apparent hold on one of his men. He hated her almost as much as he hated the female airline pilot. The one who had baited him into failure in the alley. *I will slit Kelly Hunter's throat myself and take the aircraft from her.* The pencil Atta was holding snapped in his fist and a thin trickle of blood oozed through his fingers. Marwan stared in alarm and placed a hand on his shoulder. A thin film of sweat broke out on Atta's forehead.

"Mohamed, are you well?" Marwan asked solicitously. "You must eat more." Atta took a shuddering breath and the color began returning to his features.

"I am fine Marwan." he replied. "I am just...making plans."

Three and a half hours later the cab pulled into the driveway of their rented pink stucco house. The meter read $355.00. Marwan got out. Atta had given the driver $400.00. Atta remained in the seat behind the driver and tapped him on the arm holding his hand out palm up. "What mon?" the driver asked innocently. "Dis be where you want be dropped off. Right?"

"My change." Atta stated. "I gave you four hundred American dollars". "Course yo did mon, I know dat." The Rastafarian grinned at Atta in white-toothed affability. He placed $45.00 in Atta's hand, waiting for his hard-earned tip. Atta grunted and shoved the money in his pocket. He got out of the cab without a backward glance, walked into the house and shut the door before the disgruntled driver realized what happened. When it became obvious Atta wasn't coming back, the Rastafarian stomped out of the cab and slammed his hand down on the hood in a flurry of lashing dreadlocks and garishly colored clothing. He glared at the pink house. Then he had second thoughts about the wisdom of confronting drug dealers in their lair. He finally settled on driving off in a cloud of profanity and loose gravel. *It was going to be a long expensive drive home.*

"These infidels are all thieves and liars." Atta stated wearily as he sat down at his laptop. Emotion took its toll on him. "The world will be a paradise once we rid it of this pestilence. Thieves like that will have their right hands cut off to remind them of the price to be paid for stealing in Islam."

"Allahu Akbar. His name be praised." Marwan agreed.

"I long for paradise Marwan." Atta stated in an uncharacteristic display of weakness.

"We are the beginning of the end of them Mohamed." he said reassuringly. "These people are not Allah's chosen as we are." he rationalized. "They are infidels. No better than pigs. They all need to die."

"These people" meant unbelievers as well as Muslims that did not live by Al Qaeda's radical form of Islam. Even the possibility that a few of their own innocent bystanders who did adhere to radical Islam would be killed in the coming slaughter carried no guilt for them. *"After all,"* they agreed. *"we are just sending the worthy to heaven sooner and the unworthy to Hell as Allah wills."* In the new war Bin Laden hoped to start between Muslim nations and Westernized nations, the Caliphate would only allow radical Muslims to live. Marwan felt the familiar power rush as he anticipated going out in a blaze of glory.

"You taught me that the highest level of Paradise awaits the martyrs who make great sacrifices in the name of Allah." he said, gazing fondly at Atta. Out of respect for Atta's prudish sensibilities he stopped short of mentioning the 72 virgins. Atta's mouth softened slightly as he turned and actually saw Marwan for the first time in days.

"Inshallah." he agreed. Allah's will be done. "I will stay up and fly the Microsoft 767 Simulator for a while Marwan." he stated. "Your council always refreshes me." Atta turned back to the computer. "You may bring me a cup of tea now. We will start bringing in the first of the Brigades of Belief tomorrow. I still have much work to do".

"Yes Mohamed." Marwan started toward the small grimy kitchen to do as he was told.

Chapter Twenty-Two
Flight School

*April 5, 2001 / 11:12 am PST / Montgomery
Field, San Diego California*

**"We experience moments absolutely free from
worry. These brief respites are called panic."**

-   Cullen Hightower

"Ahhhh! Ah- Allah!" A terrified voice
behind him was still screaming. The flight
instructor flinched away from the sound. He
stifled an urge to grab the control yoke as the
other Yemini yanked it spasmodically back
and forth. Sucking in a breath through
clenched teeth, the instructor thought about
his overdue mortgage payment. These
Middle Eastern men were prospective student
pilots. At this early point in their flight
training he could keep them from killing
themselves while they learned the basics.

Let him get a feel for it. the instructor
reminded himself. He surveyed the wild-eyed
man sitting next to him and tried to be
sympathetic. *These guys are from another*

culture. They barely speak English. This can't be easy for them. The Yemeni slammed the rudder controls hard left. Caught off guard, the instructor's head smacked into the right side window. He locked his feet neutrally onto the dual rudder pedals and righted the aircraft again.

"Easy Nawaf." he cautioned. "Gently. Use small movements." The view of the approaching runway settled into a slower oscillation around one area on the windscreen. Reassured, Nawaf shoved the nose down, initiating a new series of unintended aerobatics.

Another stream of Farsi erupted from Khalid as he clutched the back of the American flight instructor's right seat. Sitting through Nawafs' attempts at a landing was worse than anything Khalid had ever imagined. Nawaf had said that flying an airplane would be much like driving a car. Easy.

This is NOT like driving a car! Khalid thought, feeling betrayed. *Please Allah. I will die for you, but not like this.* He imagined them cart-wheeling down the runway in a charred ball of flames. This image was sharpened as Nawaf shoved the nose down.

"Allah! Inshallah! Aaahh!" Khalid shrieked as he floated up against his seatbelt. Scrabbling for something to hold on to, Khalid grabbed the back of their instructor's shoulder harnesses and shirt, unaware that he was choking his only hope for survival.

The flight instructor yelled "I've got it!" Neutralized the controls, and leveled the plane on glideslope again before giving the controls back to Nawaf. The three occupants of the small training aircraft were creating their own version of turbulence as they attempted to land. The day was calm and clear at Montgomery Field in San Diego. Narwaf had managed to sink below the glideslope again. He jerked the nose up to reach it.

The stall warning horn bleated along with Khalid. He squawked intermittent promises to God if only this would stop. The instructor tried to ignore it and doggedly sat on his hands as he tried to make a pilot out of Nawaf. "You're getting too slow." he cautioned. "Let the nose drop and push the power in or we'll stall."

The Yemeni shoved the throttle hard against the panel, causing the nose to pitch up even more and the airplane to shudder ominously. The flight instructor pushed forward on the yoke, slapped the Yemini's hand away from the throttle and eased the power back again. Nawaf and the instructor plunged on toward the runway in their tug of war for the flight controls. Khalid wondered if it still counted as martyrdom if he died in training. People watching the airplane from the ground waited for a disaster. The touchdown zone loomed large and threatening in the windscreen. Khalid's eyes glazed over as he prepared for the end.

The runway rose up and bounced them back into the air. Khalid had lapsed into a coma-like silence. The aircraft rebounded one last time and settled into a wobbly landing roll. Once down, a perspiring Nawaf tried to find the right braking force by stomping on and letting up on the toe brakes. It was either full on or full off with him. The little plane hiccupped down the strip and careened onto the taxiway.

The instructor was tired of having his head whipped like a yo-yo and his aircraft abused. He made it clear that Nawaf could let go. "OK Nawaf. I've got it. Get off the brakes!" Sam planted his feet firmly on the rudders and grabbed the yoke to stop the Yemini from jerking it back and forth.

"The yoke doesn't DO anything on the ground." he explained. "Don't try to steer with it." He pictured control cables fraying and rivets popping as the ailerons banged against their stops. Sam could identify with his mistreated machine. He winced and noticed that his left eye had developed a twitch.

Nawaf grinned widely. He released the controls and sat back with an expression that indicated he expected praise for a job well done. Sweat stained the armpits of his shirt and a pungent odor offered further testimony to his efforts. Sam opened a side window to air out the cockpit. He guided the little plane into its parking space and shut the engine down, promising himself that there were some things he wouldn't do for money.

"How many lessons before you put us to train big Boeings?" Nawaf asked as he leaned against the counter in the small flight school's lobby. Kahlid had not returned from the bathroom yet. The instructor motioned Nawaf to follow him into his office and eased himself into a worn pleather chair behind the desk. Sam stared at Nawaf in disbelief.

"We have money for flying Boeings." the Yemeni followed Sam waving his hands expansively. "Big jet airplanes we fly soon now, eh? Two more weeks now, eh?" The door to the men's room banged open as a green looking Khalid made his way to the lobby. Sam sighed and laid his pen down. He looked up and motioned both men to take a seat in the worn plastic chairs in front of the desk.

"Guys." he said, cradling his stubbled chin with his palm. "You can't do that no matter how much money you have. You have to go slower. Flying big jets requires much more time, training and more pilot ratings."

Nawaf and Khalid looked puzzled. They turned away and began discussing what they thought he had told them. Nawaf leaned in to the instructor with a patronizing look that said *You not understand what I want. I will say it again.*

"OK Sam." Nawaf smiled. "We fly big airplanes slower because it is easier. Big Boeings have automatic pilot. Fly easier. Slower." He turned and nodded at Khalid who nodded back. They waited expectantly for the instructor to indicate he finally understood. "We pay you now and we get Boeing pilot ratings." he added.

Sam's forehead wrinkled in exasperation. The image of a terrified and paralyzed Khalid in the pilot's seat, arms locked and feet jammed onto the flight controls immediately came to his mind. It swapped places with the more recent memory of Nawaf's manic attempts to strong-arm the airplane into submission. The flight instructor's hopes for a solution to his mortgage woes fled in the face of reality.

"No." he stated. "You guys do not fly any airplane again right now."

Nawaf and Khalid looked at each other then back to Sam. "But we have..." Nawaf began.

Sam held a protesting hand up. "I know." he said. "You have money. Your money is no good for flying now." he continued, standing up and walking over to the two men. Sam spoke in a slow deliberate manner. "English is the International language of aviation." He touched Nawaf's arm and pointed outside to the airplanes. "To fly airplanes, you must speak English." Looking at the crestfallen men, Sam explained. "You boys need to learn to speak English first and grasp a basic understanding of the ground school flight curriculum. The laws of aerodynamics. Principles of lift, drag, gravity, thrust and the airplane itself. Mother nature and the laws of God and physics don't care about your money. They don't tolerate many mistakes, ever. They'll kill you. They'll kill me and anyone else who doesn't thoroughly understand and obey them." He pointed at his mouth to emphasize what he was trying to tell them. "English first. Then you come back and I teach you to fly. Understand?" Sam thought

The laws of nature and Physics don't tolerate fools for long either. but he didn't say it.

Judging from their expressions, the instructor could tell they finally did understand. What puzzled him was the undercurrent of fear he detected in the men when it dawned on them that they were not going into big jets, or flying anything any time soon.

Mohamed el Amir Atta will NOT be happy about this. Nawaf thought. Khalid's face mirrored his fears. It was apparent this American flight instructor would not be swayed by offers of money. This was the second flight school to turn them down. Nawaf thought better of pressing the issue. He was due to call Atta tonight and advise him of their progress. Atta did not like them attracting attention to themselves. Nawaf forced himself to relax into a more congenial state.

"O.K. Sam." he smiled. "We will to do that first. We go to college and learn English good. Then we come back. Fly big Boeing jets." Khalid nodded in agreement.

Relieved, Sam smiled back and shook their hands. "You go study hard and come on back. We'll go fly together and get you working on those pilot licenses again later. OK?"

The two men nodded and headed out the doors to the parking lot. Watching them climb into their rental car and drive away, Sam sincerely hoped this would be the last he saw of them. *English or not.* he thought to himself. *If those boys get back in an airplane, they're probably going to kill themselves and anyone unfortunate enough to be riding with them.*

The drive back to their Al Qaeda financed apartment was fraught with tension between Nawaf and Khalid. Each blamed the other for what they perceived to be their partner's failure.

Later that night a disgusted Mohamed Atta placed the telephone back into its cradle with a tightly controlled rage. Marwan al-Shehhi looked up from his chapter on flight navigation and immediately knew something was wrong. "What is it Mohamed?" he asked.

"Idiots." Atta stated. "Bin Laden provides me with broken swords to fight this Jihad. Then he demands I carry it out now. Without the proper preparation!"

Marwan put his book down to give Atta his full attention.

"Nawaf and Khalid have failed another flight school and made a spectacle of themselves." Atta continued. "Nawaf spends money on sports cars, alcohol and the infidel strip clubs. Khalid is frightened of flying and screams like a woman in front of the American Instructor pilot. They disgrace us in front of our enemies." Atta took advantage of Marwan's sympathy and indulged in expressing his full frustration. "Osama seems to think he can send me sheep herders to turn into pilots. This jeopardizes our mission and depletes our funds!"

Marwan nodded and shook his head in understanding.

"You are given a task beyond bearing Mohamed." he empathized. "It is good to remember that you serve Allah and that Osama is but a tool of his will."

Atta's shoulders relaxed and he favored Marwan with a look of gratitude. "Inshallah." Atta agreed, lowering his head reverently. Marwan did the same. He was the only person that seemed to know the right thing to say to Atta. After sharing a respectful few seconds of silence with Marwan, Atta sat down and began forming a new plan.

"You are blessed with the wisdom of the prophet Marwan." he stated. "Allah's words have been sent through you to guide me. I will not fail my sacred mission. I will not bend to Bin Laden or any man." This revelation seemed to reassure Atta. He stood and turned to Marwan with a renewed sense of purpose and power.

"Bin Laden provides the money." Atta said. "He claims credit and fame as he hides in Pakistan and Afghanistan and issues Fatwas against the Great Satan. I am the one who will make these things a reality. We," Atta struck his chest emphatically with his fist, "are the Holy warriors who bring the battle to the Infidels and I am the one who will say how and when it will be done. Osama cannot do this without me."

The fanatic light that burned in Atta's eyes as he ranted caused Marwan to drop his gaze. That, and lowering his head saved Marwan from being hit in the face by spittle from Atta's fevered speech. Atta was too entranced by his own performance to notice. Marwan wisely continued crouching on the floor of their threadbare living room carpet in apparent obeisance. "Allahu Akbar. God is great." was his only comment.

Atta's breathing slowed and the flat black of his pupils returned to their normal size. He placed a hand on the top of Marwan's head in a benevolent gesture. "We have done well Marwan." he stated, counting their goals. "In six weeks, we will be taking our last pilot examinations. Then we will begin Boeing simulator training." He bared his teeth. "We know Kelley Hunter's flight schedules." Atta seemed to be talking to convince himself. He spoke of Kelly as if she were the main objective in their mission.

Marwan stood warily as Atta removed his hand and worked himself back into his former cool calculating mood.

"Yes Mohamed. We are doing as Allah wills." Marwan agreed. "You will continue to guide us well."

Atta looked around the small living space. "*Allah* guides us well." he corrected Marwan. "We needed more privacy and Allah provided it by assuring that the woman from the flight school would no longer rent to us. Now we have a house all to ourselves with no one prying into how we live, who is here or what we do."

"Surely Allah provides. His name be praised." Marwan spoke as he remembered the secretary telling them that they were too messy and would have to find another place to stay. The fact that they didn't feel the need to use air conditioning during the hot Florida summer seemed to have bothered her. *She should have been grateful to us for keeping her air conditioning bills down.* he thought. It has been the height of rudeness for her to allude to a smell in their room. He never noticed a smell. The heat was nothing compared to the heat in Egypt.

Atta turned and walked toward their tiny kitchen. "We will rest now and have tea before prayers. Then we should reward ourselves." Atta stated with uncharacteristic generosity. "We will visit the Kasbah Padeshah tonight for dinner."

Marwan smiled and relaxed. "That would be a very nice thing Mohamed." Both men usually frequented Wal Mart or Target for necessities and ate the occasional pizza there. They were frugal, and would return any unused funds to Al Qaeda before their deaths. For a special treat, they would enjoy a visit to the only Persian Restaurant within fifty miles. That was the Kasbah Padeshah restaurant, where they could speak their own language and comfortably discuss religion and politics without the worry of being overheard by unbelievers.

Marwan enjoyed the food. Atta ate little but rice. He went for the atmosphere. It reminded him that the world would soon be Fundamentalist Islamist. A Theocracy where Islamic law ruled everything, and infidels would either convert to Islam, pay tithes and function as their slaves, or be killed in ways that would publicly encourage others to submit.

Atta heated water for tea. His voice continued from the kitchen. "Things will be as I say. Khalid and Nawaf will not continue their pilot training. They are not fit for it. They will be the muscle in the cabin of the airliners. We will use the Frenchman, Moussaoui, if we have to."

A cabinet door slammed. The tinny sound of water being run into a container emanated from the next room. Atta continued his monologue. "Ziad Jarrah still fraternizes with the Americans in his classes and likes his Western wife and Western ways. I do not approve of this. He refuses to take orders from me. I will talk to Bin Laden and this will change." Marwan heard Atta slam the kettle down on the burner as he said this. "Ziad will submit to me or I will have him sent back to the training camps to learn how!"

Marwan had been aware of the growing tension between Ziad and Atta. He doubted that Bin Laden would agree with Atta's demand, but thought better of voicing his opinion. He was enjoying Atta's rare good mood too much.

"Bin Ladin has offered us an additional Saudi pilot if need be." Atta added with less certainty. Something about Bin Laden's insistence on this new pilot disturbed him. This would be the only cell member that Atta did not know and had not agreed to. Not being in complete control of himself and everyone around him made him feel vulnerable. Threatened.

Atta brought two chipped cups down from the cabinet and hesitated before setting them on the counter. *I am Allah's chosen Angel of righteous wrath.* he reassured himself. *Only a warrior as pure as I, never having been sullied by the touch or unclean thoughts of a woman, will be allowed control of this Holy mission.* Atta made a disagreeable face as he lowered two tea bags into the cups and poured hot water into them.

"Do you think we will have need of this new pilot?" Marwan asked from the other room.

"No." Atta stated flatly. "Five flights are too risky as it is. Four flights will be more manageable." *He had convinced Bin Laden not to try for ten flights. The original plan had listed five attacks on the West Coast and five on the East. It should be no problem to cut the five planned suicide missions on the East Coast to four. They all knew the attacks must occur within the same fifteen-minute time frame before the Americans became aware of what was happening and decided to fight back.*

"Then you will suggest this to Osama?" Marwan asked. "I think it is a wise choice." he added diplomatically.

Atta stared at the chipped cup with the image of a smiling purple dinosaur. The other had a picture of a female cartoon mouse in funny white gloves and a big red bow. Big black letters said "Minnie". The mouse seemed to be mocking him.

"Yes." Atta answered. "I serve Allah. Not Osama. Osama is just the financial means to an end." He piously bowed his head and added "Inshallah. Allah's will, not Osama's be done. I will tell him. I must humor him for now, but I will still tell him no."

Atta chose the "Barney" mug. He carried the other to Marwan in the living room.

Chapter Twenty-Three
Earning Her Stripes

April 15, 2001 / 04:00am EDT / DELTA Airlines
Flight Training Center / Atlanta, Georgia

"The crew is the heart of the airplane but the captain is its soul."

- Jill

Kelly twisted to the left and pulled the heavy flight case out of its slot. A spike of pain shot down her back. It was four A.M. and it had been a long, stressful night. "Damnit." she gasped, letting the bag drop. She slid back down in the captain's seat. Her Simulator Instructor flipped the last set of switches and turned on the lights. The big machine settled onto its hydraulic haunches with a lurch and a hiss.

"What's wrong?" he asked.

"I was reaching for my lost youth and tried to pull a thirty-pound flight kit out with a ten-pound muscle." she said. "That's what I get for being impatient." *If I did something serious to my back, I'm really FUBAR-ed.*

Kelly worried. *I don't want to call in sick and have to start training all over again. Not with only a few more simulators before my final check ride.*

"Take your time getting out." Vern advised. "Put some ice on your back tonight." He finished signing the logbook and commented "You're doing fine in the simulators. Judging by your written quizzes and emergencies in the SIMs, you know your stuff for the oral exam. What's stressing you out?" Kelly didn't want to think about it. She'd been hiding in her 767-training curriculum for the last four weeks. Slipping a hand between her back and the seat, she dug a knuckle into the trigger point in the knotted muscle.

"It's not the training." she said. "It's… just a personal issue that's making me into someone I don't like very much right now."

"Want to talk about it?" he asked.

"No. Thanks anyway." Kelly hesitated. "It's nothing that getting myself neutered won't cure."

"I think in your case, that would be spayed." Vern corrected her. "Why don't you just go ahead and cuss? This is a simulator. Profanity is a second language in here." He was gratified to see his comment bring a smile to her face.

"I usually try to reserve the "D" word for golf." she said. "The "S" word I'm saving in case I break out of the clouds expecting to see a runway, and see a mountain goat instead."

Vern shook his head, wondering why the personal problems always showed up when pilots went to training. It was hard enough when all they had to worry about was passing the course. Vern was attuned to his student's physical and psychological condition. It was part of making certain they had a decent shot at assimilating what he taught them. The dark smudges under Kelly's eyes concerned him. Vern assumed they were the predictable results of fatigue and the high-tension training environment.

"Need any help getting out of that seat?" he asked. "I'll take your flight kit upstairs for you. We'll make the debriefing as quick as possible."

Hoisting herself up and out of the left seat Kelly said "Thanks Vern. I'm good. I'll take you up on your offer to haul my flight kit upstairs."

Her co-pilot reached out to steady her elbow. "I'll bring some ice up to your room when we're done here." he suggested. "I'm good at applying pressure to the trigger points. That should stop the spasms."

"NO... thanks." she said, too emphatically.

He drew his hand back like it had been burned.

Kelly saw his reaction and was ashamed of herself. "Oh, for Pete's sake." she said, patting his arm. "I'm sorry. I know you didn't mean anything by it. I'm just a tired grouchy jerk right now."

"S-okay." he said, turning his back and reaching for his own flight kit.

Fine. Kelly thought *Now you're letting this alienate your first officer. The poor kid's going through a divorce, and you're feeling sorry for yourself because your date ghosted you big time and never called you back.*

Kelly knew Fletch had been far more than just a date. She felt like she'd entered the twilight zone. Some days she found herself wondering if the man had ever existed outside of her imagination. *He might as well have vanished off the face of the earth.*

When she wasn't feeling abandoned, she found herself being worried sick that something bad had happened to him. His phone had been disconnected. She had no way of knowing if he was dead or alive. Being stalked by Middle Eastern men on a federal watch list didn't help her feel any less paranoid. *Why did Fletch leave me hanging out to dry? Especially on this issue?* she wondered.

It's not something the man I thought I knew would do. He told me to trust him. she argued with herself. Kelly made up illogical excuses for Fletch. Then she came full circle back to feeling just plain stupid. *Has the whole world gone crazy?* she wondered, looking at her wounded co- pilot. *Or is it just me?*

"Thanks." she managed a smile. "I think I'll take you up on that ice. I won't bite your head off this time."

"Rank has its privileges captain." Her co-pilot said graciously. "Good simulator partners are hard to come by. I don't want to have to break in a new one. I'll knock and leave the ice bucket outside your door."

"Thanks kiddo. That would be great." Kelly replied.

"Fuhgeddaboudit." he replied, waving his hand dismissively. His grin told her the fences had been mended. He followed Vern up the stairs to the debriefing room.

I need to keep my emotions out of my training. Kelly reprimanded herself. *Just one more hour in the debriefing room and I can go to the hotel, a hot bath and bed.* THAT had motivational appeal. *Then I'll get up for six hours of review and study before doing it all over again.* she thought.

Kelly rubbed her eyes. She'd been assigned the dreaded middle of the night "D" period in the busy simulator sessions. The few hours Kelly did manage to sleep, she dreamed of 767 aircraft systems, Federal Aviation laws and regulations, handling multiple emergencies and complicated approach and departure procedures.

Yawning, she looked around her. Kelly felt like she'd spent half of her professional life in this building. Always training. Always being tested. Always upgrading. Some were her choice. Some were 6-month recurrent training requirements.

It was dark and cool here. The massive heat generating electronic simulator components and rows of 5-foot-tall banks of computers needed cold air. She'd been too hot during the simulator session. Now she was chilled.

Five truck-sized simulators were swaying and bobbing on their huge hydraulic legs. Mechanical hisses and groans gave the machines the illusion of being alive. They reminded her of the Imperial Walkers in the old Star Wars movies.

Kelley stared blankly at them, mesmerized by the motion. Every SIM was responding to the sets of emergencies the pilots inside were battling. Their performances were being recorded on a computer for future evaluation. Kelly shook herself, glad her session was finally over. *Five down and three more to go.* she counted, sympathizing with the pilots still inside their boxes. *A mistake that'll kill you in an airplane isn't going to kill you in a simulator.* she thought.

"Hey Kelly. How'd it go in there?" a gravelly voice from above asked.

She looked up. The next shift for the simulator was coming down the metal stairway. They'd be practicing the same maneuvers she had just completed.

"Piece-of-cake." Kelly responded with the customary bravado.

The heavy-set pilot from her ground training class put his flight case down. He looked fresher than she felt. Kelly took a peek behind him.

"Where's your partner?" she asked.

"He was having a hard time passing the oral examination." the man replied, looking grim. "Particularly with the electrical and pneumatic systems. He never made it to simulators." The big man shrugged, breaking a moment of uncomfortable silence. *Their lives might not be on the line here, but their careers were, and they all knew it.*

"John's been fighting a bad case of the flu. He finally went home sick." he continued. "I think the pressure wore him down." He gestured over his shoulder at a slim man coming out of the briefing room. "Now I've got a new partner to train."

"Bummer." Kelly said. "Good luck".

"Thanks." He looked at his new partner. "I may need it. I've never seen that guy before."

Before he disappeared into the simulator Kelly whispered a suggestion. "When your instructor gives you the Canarsie Approach you'll get a left engine fire. Look out for the missed approach procedure. The fine print tells you it's not the same with an engine out." He brightened and nodded. What she'd just told him would make him look like Sky King in his session.

"Thanks for the heads up." he grinned.

She felt good about that. "Cooperate and graduate." she acknowledged.

"Are you O.K. down there Kelly?"

Her co-pilot stuck his head out of the debriefing room. "Vern says to get up here."

Kelly turned and climbed up the last few steps. "Don't beat this tired old body. I'm coming." she said, poking fun at her own misery. The first officer snorted and turned to repeat her comment to the instructor.

"She's coming boss. Don't beat her up any more tonight."

Kelly was back in her room at the Holiday Inn by five-thirty am. A thin glow of light painted the horizon. She closed the blackout curtains and crawled into bed to hide from it. A warm bath had relaxed her knotted muscles. The bag of ice was wrapped in a towel and packed against her back. Kelly pulled a pillow over her head to block out the light and the noise of the awakening hotel. Burnt toast smells wafted up from the coffee shop. She was dead to the world in minutes. It was more like passing out than falling asleep. Blessedly, there were no dreams.

Kelly woke up curled into a fetal position around her pillow. Miraculously, nothing hurt. She'd forgotten how nice a few hours of uninterrupted sleep felt. Reluctant to pass back into the realities of her world, Kelly tucked her nose into the pillow and snuggled deeper under the covers. Drifting in that soft space between sleep and wakefulness, she breathed in the fresh clean scent of rain. The smooth feel of warm skin seemed to caress her. Kelly hugged the comforting presence in her arms closer.

She opened her eyes to the empty hotel room. Large digital numbers on the clock next to the bed read 1:00 pm. Thunder boomed outside. *"No fair sneaking up on me like that Fletcher."* she muttered to no-one. Rolling over, her back met the unpleasant damp sensation of a bag of ice that had leaked into the towel. She groaned and moved away from the offending wet spot. *It was Ground Hog Day again.*

Kelly sighed and stared at the ceiling, arching her back slightly to test it. A warning pang tweaked back at her. Kelley wished she could manage a good work out. She had some self-inflicted frustrations to burn off.

Time for a reality check. she decided. I can't keep living like this. *Fletch dropped me from his life for reasons I'll probably never understand... I suppose that's his prerogative.* Kelley rationalized. *It's without compassion or consideration, but that seems to be the way people treat each other these days, - Move on and get over it.* she told herself harshly.

I expected better of him... The thought crept unbidden into her mind. To her dismay, she felt tears welling in her eyes. Kelly wiped them away with the back of her hand and sat up. *If I have control of nothing else,* Kelley decided. *I can at least control my attitude.* She could choose to believe that Fletch was never the man she thought he was and her time with him was a lie, or she could do what he asked and trust him. As far as Kelly was concerned, the first choice wasn't an option. To see him in that light was unbearable.

Keep the memories and move on. she told herself. It took a conscious effort for her to stop asking herself why and to quash the constant feeling that she was being hunted.

Kelly decided to handle one problem at a time. Her immediate concern was getting through 767 training. "Well then." she said to no one in particular. "Let's get back to the books. If you're going to be a captain on this bird you'd better start acting like one."

Chapter Twenty-Four
The Good Soldier

*May 1, 2001 / 09:00am GMT / London
Heathrow International Airport / London,
England*

**"My mind is a dangerous neighborhood. I
should not wander in there alone."**

- Anonymous

Union Jacks splashed red, white, and blue colors along the tail of the BOAC 747 that taxied into the gate beside them. Animal winced at the noise and programmed the last few coordinates into the navigation system of his Delta 767-ER. The transoceanic flight from Heathrow to JFK would be a long one. He'd visited a few pubs the day before. After tossing darts with the locals for two hours, he'd finally managed to get a few hours of sleep.

"Coffee?" A very British flight attendant entered the cockpit. Animal reached for the cup.

"Thanks. This jet lag has me so far behind myself I could pick my own pocket."

I know what you mean, ducks." she agreed. "A nice brekkie of bangers and mash and a good blood puddin' always sets me to rights." She handed him his beverage. "Can I get you some?"

"Are you kidding'?" he asked, turning a slight shade of green. "I never eat anything with the word "blood" in it. I'll have what I brought with me." He pulled out a big bag of Southern fried 'Chitlins.

"Suit yourself luv." she made a face at the fried desiccated pig intestines and turned toward the cockpit door. "We've got a Federal Air Marshal back here wanting to introduce himself."

"Bring him on up. The captain's down in dispatch. He'll be back in a minute." Animal focused his attention on the cellophane. It was resisting his attempts to rip it open with his teeth.

"See you later then." she replied, edging out the door and motioning the Air Marshal forward.

"Mmmph.." he answered amiably, still wrestling with the bag. It finally surrendered. He reached in and grabbed his prize.

"Sir? A quiet voice behind him caught his attention.

That was quick. Animal thought, turning in his seat and rolling his eyes up to see who'd spoken. A slender man with an athletic build smiled down at him. The man's high cheekbones and golden skin hinted at Native American stock, but his deep blue eyes indicated a blend of European as well.

"Eugene Fletcher." he said, opening his jacket to take his FAM credentials from the inner pocket. He almost laughed at the sight of the tough looking co-pilot with a mouth full of cellophane and a hand full of deep-fried pig guts.

Animal's gaze swiveled from the man's face down to a gleam of gold from something pinned inside his jacket. "Whuff's that?" he asked, spitting the scrap of cellophane out and pointing to the object. Fletch looked down at the wings he'd been wearing over his heart for the last several months. "Those are a Delta Pilot's wings." Animal said, answering his own question. "How'd you get a pair?" He thought he saw a flicker of pain cross the man's features.

"A good…friend of mine. A Delta Pilot gave them to me." Fletch said, taking his credentials out and closing his jacket. I haven't seen her in quite a while." he added. Fletch hesitated on the "friend" part. *What must she think of me now?* he wondered miserably.

"Her?" Animal conjectured, putting the pieces together. "You don't mean Kelley Hunter do you?" he asked. "We don't have many female pilots. That stinker told me she lost her wings." Animal studied Fletch speculatively. "We're not supposed to give those away unless it's to another pilot when they upgrade. You've got to be pretty special if she gave you her wings." he finished.

"How is she?" *Surely there's no harm in asking about her.* Fletch thought.

"Come to think of it, I saw her in training a few weeks ago." Animal shook his head. "She was pretty subdued for Kelley. - Didn't say much. She looked tired and kind of sick, like she'd lost her best friend or something. Training will do that to you." he concluded. "It can get pretty stressful, but she'll make it. She's a smart cookie and a good stick."

That wasn't what Fletch wanted to hear, but a small selfish part of him was glad she missed him so much.

"You know what's funny?" The First Officer continued. "If you hadn't been a Federal Air Marshal with those Delta Pilot wings I might have thought you were part of the group that's been stealing our uniforms and badges on layovers."

"What?" Fletcher's instinctive alarms went on high alert. "Is that still happening?"

Animal shrugged. "I know it doesn't make any sense, but Delta put out another new security bulletin warning flight crews that someone's been taking our uniforms, our credentials and our badges out of hotel rooms." he guffawed. "Now what would anybody want with stuff like that? You can't sell it for anything." The first officer stopped laughing when he saw the look on the Air

Marshal's face. "You don't look so good yourself. Can I get you a bottle of water?" he asked. "Chitlins?" he offered solicitously, holding out the bag of delicacies.

"No thanks." Fletch said distractedly. "I'd like copy of that new security bulletin if you have a spare."

"Heck, take mine." Animal offered, digging in his flight kit. "I already know what it says."

Fletch took the paper from Animal, folded it, and put it in his pocket. He'd review it on the flight back to New York. "I appreciate that." Fletch responded. "I don't think I caught your name First Officer….?"

Animal filled in the blanks. "Amos Nathanial Lander. You can call me Animal. Everyone else does." He grinned through a mouthful of Southern fried treats and offered Fletch his hand. "I got that nick-name in the military and it's stuck ever since. Never could understand why."

"A pleasure to meet you Animal." Fletch said, shaking co-pilot's hand and grinning in spite of himself. "I'll be back in seat 3C. The captain can call me if he wants to contact us."

"I'll tell him." Animal assured Fletch. "I'll also tell Kelley you said hello." Seeing the pained look on Fletcher's face he added "Or not."

Fletch hesitated, considering his options and their consequences. He chose the one he could live with. "I'd like a moment to speak with you privately regarding Kelly when we get to New York." Fletch said. "I know this is a long flight and you'll be tired, but it's important."

"Not a problem." Animal assured him. "You've got me curious now."

"Great." Fletch grinned. "I'll see you on the ground in New York." His pulse accelerated. The certainty of what he had to do pounding through his veins as he turned and walked back to First Class. People were putting luggage in the overhead bins and settling down for the long flight. Fletcher scanned them automatically. Sorting appearance, body language and actions for irregular or red flag behavior. His conscious mind was already at work on the escalating threat to Kelley and the airlines. The new information Animal had unwittingly provided made Fletcher's hackles rise. Whatever had been going on in February was still in place and accelerating.

Two hours later, the other passengers had pulled down the window shades and were enjoying the in-flight movie. Fletcher was one of the few who still had his overhead light on. The Delta Security bulletin Animal had given him was short and concise. It did little more than confirm what the first officer had already told him. That was more than enough to get his mind going on a multitude of possibilities. All of them led him back to the same unthinkable conclusion. *These guys are planning on taking control of a commercial aircraft. Some by impersonating pilots or flight attendants.* Fletch realized. *If they're doing that, they don't intend to let the flight crew live.* Fletch put the bulletin down and took a sip of ice water. His throat had gone dry. Atta's willingness to risk his cover to get to Kelly made it clear that he intended to make her part of his plan. This fell in line with the NSA Officer's order to leave Kelley out there as bait. To tell her nothing, and to break all contact with her with no goodbyes. No explanations. Nothing. His eyes widened as he stared at the notification and recalled what had finally convinced him to be "the good soldier." At the time, Lt. Colonel Joe Johnson had made a persuasive argument on Kelley's behalf. "If her airline gets wind of the attention she's drawing from terrorists, how long do you think they'll allow her to keep her job?" he'd asked. "Their legal and training departments have ways of getting rid of pilots they don't want." That, and the idea that he'd be useless to her if he lost his job and security clearance was all that kept Fletch from picking up the phone and calling Kelley.

Fletcher had found and torn out the bugs the NSA Intelligence officer ordered to be placed in his living quarters when he and Kelly had been together. Fletch waited for the disciplinary phone call after clearing them out. It never came. *That either meant they'd lost interest in him, or they'd replaced the devices. He didn't care anymore.* Fletch realized he'd already chosen his course of action when he asked Animal for a private chat in JFK. That decision lifted a weight from his shoulders. He felt free again.

"Ma'am?" he addressed a passing flight attendant. "I think I'll take you up on lunch after all."

"Certainly sir." she smiled. "We have Yorkshire pudding or Kidney Pie."

"Yorkshire Pudding." he said without hesitation.

"I'll have that right up. Would you like a wine list?"

"No thanks. Orange juice will be fine." Fletch watched her walk up the aisle as a male flight attendant passed down the adjoining walkway. *It could be either one of them.* he realized uneasily. *For that matter, it could even be the captain he hadn't met.* Those were thoughts he didn't want to dwell on.

Fletch pulled out his palm pilot and started reviewing his resources. Old friends who owed him a few favors. New friends who would want to help and a variety of data banks he was still privy to. Some things were easy enough for anyone to check on-line.

It will just take a little time and knowing where to look. Fletch thought. He was good at that. An individual always worked faster, cleaner, and more imaginatively than a bureaucracy. As far as he knew, Kelley was still safe on the ground in training, and he had his own ways of finding Atta and his group.

Fletch made a note to himself, "*Check out all flight schools in the US with foreign students of Middle Eastern origin in the last two years.*" Logic told him their focus on aircraft and impersonating pilots indicated they might try to take a little flight training to fit in. They might even have a need to use it.

The United States was the flight training Mecca for the world. It was a good bet they'd be doing it here. The more he thought about it, the more likely it seemed. By the time his meal arrived Fletch had a list of contacts long enough to bear fruit and keep him busy following up on leads. His appetite was back and his fingers itched to call Kelley, explaining everything, making it all right again. Something told him *"Not yet."*

He settled for devouring his first meal in a day.

Chapter Twenty-Five
Secret Squirrel

May 1, 2001/ 11: 45am EST / JFK International Airport

"*The psychological pressure on an operative deployed covertly is enormous.*"

- George Friedman – Author
"America's Secret War"

"Please turn off all electronic devices and return your seat backs and tray tables to their original upright and locked positions." the flight attendant's landing mantra continued. Fletch leaned over to the window and watched the Hudson River glitter a welcome home. He could see the tiny form of the Statue of Liberty dwarfing ships arriving at the mouth of the river, and the Island of Manhattan with its two trademark towers rising above the city.

The big jet rolled level, providing him with a view of New York. It reminded him that this was the last known whereabouts of Mohamed Atta. *I'll check the FAA's student pilot and pilot database first.* he decided. *That should give me the names and flight school locations.* Once Fletch focused on a target it consumed him. *They move around.* he decided. *Atta's not in Seattle or New Jersey any more.*

Wind noise and a reassuring rumble announced the gear falling into place as they descended over the Atlantic Ocean in preparation for the final approach to landing. A smiling flight attendant passed down the aisle collecting the long day's detritus. Fletch realized he could never overlook the flight crews again. They had seemed to be a reliable part of the aircraft before. More like functioning pieces of equipment than individuals. The Security Bulletin put flight crews in a whole new light.

The last cup was picked up and the cabin crew sat down just before they rolled the wheels onto the runway. Jumbo jets from a variety of exotic countries threaded themselves into the line of U.S. air carriers ringing the terminal buildings.

Passengers raced each other to stand up and retrieve their belongings when they blocked in at the gate. Fletch remained seated. He'd already told his partner to go on without him. When the aisles had finally cleared, he got up and walked to the flight deck.

Animal was sitting alone in the cockpit.

"I told the captain I'd see him downstairs. Didn't have to tell him twice either." he grinned. "He was tired."

Fletch grinned back. "Good work. I get the feeling people tend to underestimate you."

"All of the time, but it works in my favor." Animal acknowledged. Gesturing to the jump seat behind the captain's chair, he said "Have a seat. Close the door and tell me what I can do for you."

Fletch heard the cockpit door click into place as he closed it and sat down. "How well do you know First Officer Hunter? he asked.

The co-pilot looked puzzled at the question. "First off." he began. "It's probably Captain Kelley Hunter by now. We've flown together quite a bit on other aircraft. She's one of our best pilots. On a personal level, my wife and I also consider her a good friend." He looked at Fletch. "If you don't mind my saying so, I get the feeling you and Kelley are more than just good friends."

Fletch wondered how the tables had been turned on him so adeptly. He'd gone from being the interrogator to the subject in a few well-placed sentences from the deceptively simple looking co-pilot. That made Fletch more comfortable with the favor he was about to ask of the man.

"To say that I care a great deal about Kelley would be an understatement." Fletch admitted. "I think she also cares about me. Right now, she probably doesn't have very high opinion of me."

Animal glowered at Fletch, his expression as much saying *"What did you do to her, you jerk?"*

Fletch raised a hand in defense. "It's not what you, or Kelley think." he stated. "Far from it." He looked down at his clasped hands. Then he raised his head and looked straight at the first officer. "Animal, I would do anything to protect that lady. I find myself caught in the crossfire of security issues and my feelings for her. This could cost me more than my job if it isn't kept strictly confidential and it would be a risk to Kelley herself." Fletch saw the skepticism in the co-pilot's eyes and answered the question before it could be asked.

"I'm not doing anything illegal, unethical or contrary to this country's security. Quite the opposite." he added. "This is one of those times when the bureaucracy rolls over issues that need to be pursued. I'm afraid Kelley might end up as part of the collateral damage. I was given direct orders to have no further contact with her, and it's killing me, but I won't let her down."

"I'm listening." Animal replied, his expression softening. "Go on."

"I guess you'll just have to trust me on this. My intentions are to pursue leads on a set of circumstances that may affect her. I don't think the Feds are doing this. I want to keep track of her flight schedules as well. It's the only way I can make sure she's not headed for something ... bad."

"What do you mean by bad?" Animal asked, his jaw jutting out defiantly.

" Very possibly life and death bad. I don't know the exact form of the threat yet, but I'm convinced some bad actors are targeting her in their as yet, unknown plans." Fletch answered. "Even if I did …"

"I know. I know." Animal replied. "If ya' told me you'd have to kill me. Secret squirrel stuff. Skip it."

Fletch smiled gratefully. "Thanks. I'm trusting you to keep this strictly between the two of us, if you' re willing to help me."

Animal looked him up and down appraisingly before answering. "Normally I'd say you're just another guy up to no good, but if Kelley thought so highly of you she gave you her wings, that's good enough for me." Animal made sure the cockpit voice recorder circuit breaker was pulled, leaned forward and asked "What can I do to help?"

Fletch knew he'd just gained a valuable ally. "Here's a secure phone number you can reach me at." he said, handing Animal a slip of paper. "Give me a way of contacting you.

I'll have a Post Office Box where you can send me copies of Kelley's flight schedules when you get them. That will be a great help, and a great relief to me knowing where she is. I'll be working on the other problem in the meantime. Sorry I can't tell you more."

"Maybe later when it's not secret squirrel stuff anymore we can both sit down and have a couple of beers and laughs over it." Animal suggested, taking the paper.

"I'll look forward to it." Fletch responded.

Animal handed Fletch a card with his address and cell phone number. "Maybe I ought to get some other cards made up with *Secret Agent Animal* on them. -Just joking." he added, throwing his hands up palms forward for emphasis.

"That's the down side of the secret squirrel business." Fletch responded. "No one ever knows the good deeds you've done."

Fletch stood up and held out his hand. Animal got out of his seat and shook it firmly. "Let me know if there's anything else I can do." he said seriously.

"Just stay close to her if you can." Fletch said. "Keep in touch. You're helping more than you know. Thank you." he added. "I look forward to buying those beers."

"All this intrigue and free beer too?" Animal remarked. "This job was getting too tame anyway. I'll hold you to it."

Fletch picked up his luggage and turned to leave.

"Look after her." He reiterated.

"As best I can." Animal reassured him. "I'll try to buddy bid her trips with her."

Fletch turned and walked into the terminal to catch his flight back to Washington D.C. He had a lot of work to do when he got there, but it was work he was champing at the bit to begin. He had a sense that Kelley's time was running out.

Chapter Twenty-Six
Check Your Six

May 1, 2001 / 3:15pm EST / Delta flight training center / Atlanta, Georgia

"Worrying is not an option. It is a responsibility."

- NAN

"If you find yourself in a situation where your aircraft is hijacked, do not resist." The Delta Airlines security instructor tapped his pointer on the chalkboard for emphasis. The faces of the pilots in his class registered everything from pragmatic acceptance to suppressed outrage. "If they want to come into the cockpit," he continued. "Let them in. If they want to go somewhere, take them there." Kelley's hand flew up at the back of the classroom. "Yes, Captain Hunter?" he acknowledged. "Do you have a question?"

"Yes sir." Kelley lowered her hand and asked "What if the hijackers are killing my passengers or crew? Do I remain passive?"

"That's the point Kelley." he said, facing his students. "If you don't resist and you give them what they want there will be no casualties. If you do resist, the odds are it will be disastrous. It's pure human psychology."

He bounced the pointer in his hand and resumed his pacing. "This is the official common strategy used by all U.S. Air Carriers. It's based on the fact that no one wants to die. Self-preservation wins out every time." Most of the class looked hopeful, or resigned. A few doubting faces still peppered his audience. "If they kill the pilots, they die too. Do what they say. Take them where they want to go, and don't fight it. Cooperate and everyone will be just fine."

Kelly nodded. She understood the rationale behind what the instructor was saying, but couldn't help feeling it was incredibly naive.

"Yeah Kelley. Submit and do what they say." a rugged senior captain at the front teased. "Not everybody's a black belt looking for bad guys to practice on. The rest of us have to whimper and beg for mercy."

"Thank you for your support, Captain Jack." the instructor acknowledged. When the laughter died down' he continued. "There's one exception to what I've just told you. If you draw some nut case that wants to die, all bets are off." The room went quiet except for an occasional nervous shuffling of paper.

"What do we do then?" the pilot sitting next to Kelley asked.

"I'm afraid there is no set answer." the instructor replied. "You're going to have to determine that for yourselves, if and when the time comes. The chances of that ever happening are slim and none." he added reassuringly. "Talk to them and try to calm them down. Show them pictures of your kids. Humanize yourself."

The faces he saw as he looked out on his class had lost their good-natured demeanor. Each one was asking himself the same question. *What will I, or can I do if the hijacker wants to die?*

"I don't know about the rest of you guys," Captain Jack replied. " I'm going to bid back to co-pilot and fly with Kelley." The remark broke the tension and relieved laughter spilled out.

"Thank you again Captain Jack." the instructor said.

"Captain Hunter. It looks like your dance card's filled with this cowardly older-than-dirt soon to be co-pilot again here."

"I think I'm safe." Kelley replied. "Captain Jack's got too many ex-wives to support to go back to first officer pay." This time the class roared at the rough old captain's expense. He laughed with them.

"Moving right along," the instructor continued. "We can probably get out of here tonight at four o'clock instead of five if you guys want to waive your breaks and keep on going." A room full of hopeful faces shown up at him. "Or," he suggested. "We can break for fifteen minutes now and get out at five as scheduled."

"Keep going!" the group yelled.

"O.K." he continued. "As far as possible threats go, the only thing we have on the radar is a Saudi guy called Osama bin Laden." Noting the blank looks, he continued. "We suspect Bin Laden may have had something to do with the bombing of the U.S. Cole in the Middle East in December, and American embassy bombings in Nairobi, Kenya, and Tanzania in 1998. Now he's shown some interest in the airlines." A clueless silence descended on the room.

"So, we look for guys with beards, scimitars and long white robes named Bin Laden?" the pilot next to Kelley commented. She could identify with his frustration. The instructor gave him a long-suffering look. "I'm serious." the co-pilot continued. With due respect, all we've got is a weird name we've never heard of belonging to some guy in the Middle East who likes to blow up boats and embassies and might want to play with airplanes." He looked around at his classmates. "What do we do with that information?"

"Just be aware of it." the instructor replied. " And try not to look like you're profiling Middle Eastern men while you're doing it. It's not politically correct and our legal department will have a fit if they think you are. Now you know as much as I do."

"And give Bin Laden what he wants." the pilot sitting next to Captain Jack added, nudging him in the ribs.

"Stop asking questions and maybe we'll still get out of here at four thirty." the captain behind him grumbled. "I have a plane to catch." Cowed, the first officer crossed his arms and closed his mouth. It was obvious they had all the information they were going to get.

Kelley's mind slipped back to the Middle Eastern faces she'd identified in Fletcher's photo gallery. She wondered if Bin Laden had anything to do with them. *My mind wonders too many things, too often.* she told herself, banishing the image of Fletch racing through the fog to her rescue. *I just want to get back home, see my son, sleep in my own bed and get back to flying the line.* She smiled at the prospect and her thoughts returned to the security issue.

If all those guys want is to hijack my plane and go somewhere, I guess I can live with that. She decided. *I don't have to like it, but I can live with it. I'll even give them extra bags of peanuts, just to keep them happy.*

Kelly found herself grinding her teeth at the idea. Letting people with bad intentions take over her airplane, crew and passengers went against her grain.

Six weeks had passed since Kelley arrived in Atlanta to begin training. The 767/757 dual captain's type ratings were added to her license and her flight home would be leaving in two hours. It was finally over.

Kelly smiled to herself. *Home in May.* She thought. *Just in time to see our fruit trees in full bloom.* She pictured the deep pink and white flower petals swirling in the spring breeze like confetti. That pleasant picture was marred by a small voice nagging at the back of her mind. *Watch your six.* it persisted. *Something bad is closing in on you. You're on your own.* The voice wouldn't shut up. Kelley sighed and realized she was also very tired.

Chapter Twenty-Seven
Gone Hunting

*July 26, 2001 / 03:00 am EST /
Washington, DC*

**"*The official theory is wrong. I know
that; but how do we prove it?*"**

-Sherlock Holmes

"There you are you S.O.B." Fletcher spoke out loud, staring at the name on his computer screen. He lowered his face to rub his eyes with his fingertips.

Rocking back in his chair, he looked at the clock on the corner of the display. It was three am. A muffled boom of thunder promised some relief from the muggy weather. *Don't get excited.* he cautioned himself. *This is almost too easy. There must be a thousand guys named Mohamed in the state of Florida alone, and more than a few Attas. Not so many with pilot licenses in this time-period though.* He couldn't believe the name listed on the F.A.A. licensed pilots list was actually "Mohamed Atta." Looking for

Atta under his own name was a chance he'd taken, because it was the only option he had. It was paying off. *He's hiding in plain sight.* Fletcher realized. *What better way to avoid detection when technically, you haven't done anything wrong? Yet.*

The address given on the pilot certificate was listed in Norman, Oklahoma. So was a disconnected cell phone billing address in Atta's name. The convoluted trail led Fletcher back to Huffman Aviation, located at Venice Municipal Airport in Florida. That was the Flight School where the certificate had been issued, and it had been issued recently. Fletch bent to look at his work schedule. *Two days off starting tomorrow.* he noted. *I could use a day off Florida.* he thought. Knowing it would be anything but a day off.

Printing out the information, Fletch clicked on the internet and started looking up airline flight schedules and rental car agencies. He booked himself on the first early morning flight to Tampa, Florida. He could rent a car and drive the rest of the way to Huffman Aviation in Venice, Florida on Map Quest. He'd make it a short round-trip, and return to DC on the red eye flight this evening. Some things couldn't be done over the phone. That was a given. He had to be certain this Mohamed Atta was the same man he'd dealt with in Seattle. He needed a witness at Huffman Aviation to verify Atta's identity with his photo. *Atta might still be there, if my luck holds.* Fletch thought.

Fletcher's sources in the CIA and other Intelligence Agencies were being overwhelmed. Over a thousand information bits and vague threats were flooding into the FBI during the last few months. They hinted at multiple spectacular attacks, but were maddeningly short on actionable details. This information and the ominous increase in suspected terrorist chatter alarmed him. He forced himself to stay patient and methodical.

I can get a couple of hours of sleep before my flight leaves at 06:55. he decided. Fletch stood and stretched the stiffness out. Heading for the bedroom, he scooped up his bow and arrow as he moved. Without stopping, he knocked the arrow, drew the bow, and released in one smooth motion. He was rewarded with a sizzling sound and firm "thunk" as the head buried itself, dead-center in the target. "Got-cha'," Fletch whispered, laying the bow down and padding to his bed. *I should visualize the red dot between Atta's eyes more often.* he thought.

It was July 26, 2001, 11:30 am in Venice, Florida. The secretary behind the desk at Huffman Aviation sat the container of lasagna she'd brought from home down next to the phone. The door to the flight school opened, accompanied by ramp noise and the cough and whirr of a Cessna engine starting.

Can I help you?" She looked up and appraised the man standing in front of her. She sat straighter and smoothed her hair, smiling approvingly.

"I certainly hope so." the man smiled back. "Would you mind helping me out with a few questions?"

"Of course." she replied, anticipating a new student pilot. She hoped he'd be staying for all his pilot ratings. "How can I be of assistance?" *It's going to be so much more pleasant looking into beautiful blue eyes like his every day.* she thought. It had been a relief when the group of Islamic men, especially the one with the disturbing stare, had finally left.

"I'm trying to find out where I can contact some students of yours." Fletch replied. "Do any of these gentlemen look familiar? He spread photos of the men out on her desk. To her dismay, the secretary found herself looking into the same shark-like eyes again. She pointed to Atta. "This one I do. Is he a friend of yours?" she asked. Her tone clearly indicated she hoped he wasn't.

"No." Fletch answered truthfully. "I don't think he'd consider me a friend. If he asks, just tell him a man was here to see him about winning the Publisher's Clearing House Sweepstakes."

"He WON that?" she asked incredulously.

"Only if he asks." Fletch replied cryptically. "Do you recognize any of these other men?"

The secretary's gaze slowly shifted from Fletch back to the photos. "No. I don't recognize anyone else in these three photos." Fletch could almost see the wheels turning in her head as she started connecting the dots. " I don't recognize these two men, but Mr. Atta was here for quite some time training with a group of men that looked like them. They all had Middle Eastern names. They were foreign students getting their pilot licenses here." She'd obviously said something that piqued the good-looking gentleman's interest. She liked helping him. "I rented a room to Mr. Atta and his friend, Mr. Shehhi for a few weeks, but they were too dirty. They were ruining my carpets and attracting cockroaches. I had to ask them to leave." she continued.

"Do you know where they are now?" Fletch asked.

"I think they moved to a little pink stucco house in Nokomis for the rest of their stay. It's a rental. I felt a little guilty giving them a referral." She added. "Nokomis is the next town north of here."

"Would you have that address?" Fletch asked.

She smiled slyly. "I'm also the school's bookkeeper. It just so happens I do have that address for billing purposes." She swiveled her chair to the P.C. "Give me a second. I'll get it for you."

"That would be a great help." Fletch was astounded his good fortune. "If you happen to have the names of the men Mr. Atta was training with, can I get a copy of those as well?" he pressed.

"I don't see why not." she replied, concentrating on the screen. "There." she said proudly, hitting the print key and smiling at Fletch "You'll have it in a minute."

"Thank you." Fletcher decided to request the Nokomis city records to find the owner of the rental when he got back to D.C. He didn't have time to check it out today.

"You know." she said, glancing over her shoulder. "There is really no love lost between Mr. Atta and this flight school or I wouldn't have given you this information."

"Really?" Fletch asked, pulling up a chrome-legged chair and sitting down. "Why is that?"

"To begin with, they got us in quite a bit of trouble with the F.A.A. Atta and his buddy left one of our rental aircraft on a taxiway at Miami International when their engine quit. It was due to operator error. Not our maintenance." she was quick to add. "Then they flooded the engine trying to re-start it and left it there. It caused a mess with other planes trying to get in and out."

"Didn't the F.A.A. go after them?" he asked.

"No. The F.A.A. expects a certain number of screw-ups with foreign students learning to fly. They just fined them. Our school has a good relationship with the FAA. We straightened it out." Seeing the disapproval in Fletchers eyes, she added. "Maybe they'll mess up again. Mr. Atta passed all of his tests with flying colors, but this was a rookie mistake."

He had to smile at her eagerness to please. Standing up, he took the printout from her and spoke reassuringly. "You've been a great help. I only came in for the day. I'm catching a flight back to DC in a few hours. If I have any more questions I'll come back to

Huffman Aviation when I have a few days off." He looked at the clock on the wall and glanced at her container lasagna lunch. "If it's around lunch, next time, I'll buy."

She brightened. "Come back any time." As he turned to go, she winked and added "Good luck on the sweepstakes."

Chapter Twenty-Eight
Trouble in Paradise

August 16, 2001/ 12:46pm EST / Nokomis, Florida

"If you're in a fair fight, you didn't plan it properly."

- Nick Lappos, Chief R&D Pilot, Sikorsky Aircraft

I have made it clear that we cannot target the White House with a fifth plane, yet he continues to insist! Atta rubbed his face with both hands. *It's chaos!* he thought. The word filled his head like a mushrooming migraine. It described the fragile plan he was trying to hold together. Sheik Omar had sent the coded command from Osama bin Laden via the internet chat room. Atta hesitated before responding, afraid of what he might say. *Osama's Saudi ego will ruin us all!* Atta worried. *The White House is too well defended. One more plane is too many to manage without something going wrong.*

Atta had made the argument many times, but Osama's personal agenda kept getting in the way. Bin Laden was one of fifty sons of a wealthy Saudi. He'd been disowned after attempting a family coup. Ironically, Bin Laden was supported, trained and supplied with weapons by the US government where he had been hailed as a freedom fighter when he was fighting the Russians in Afghanistan. Now he was the money machine and force behind the attacks on America. Targeting the White House was his way of reclaiming his power and influence in the Muslim world. This last persistent demand made Atta lose the respect he'd once had for the man. It was insane. He considered the wording of his reply.

Their code for the movements of terrorists and planned attack was based on the ruse that they were all students or tourists on Visas in America. The "*University*" referred to Al Qaeda. *"Professors"* were the pilots, and *"students"* were the muscle that would prevent interference from the passengers or crew.

Atta steeled himself and attacked the keyboard again. "It is too late to change the curriculum now." Atta jabbed the keys in frustration. "Tell Osama the students and professors already have their training. The additional curriculum he asks me for is too difficult. If he insists, they will fail."

The screen remained blank for a moment. Then a line of type appeared in reply. "I will inform Osama of your decision." the message ticked out. Before he could answer another line appeared. "Your assigned homework is to study chapter five, line four. Please inform the University when the First Semester is to begin. Osama is most anxious that it occur soon."

The Jihadi leader's jaw tightened. What Omar had just told him was to "Obey God and his messenger, (Bin Laden) and not to argue about it." It was a text that Omar himself had written for the Martyrs to read on their last night on earth.

Atta decided to change his tactics. He'd give them something they wanted to distract them from the idea of adding a fifth plane. *If the holy event is to succeed,* he thought *I must set the time now before Osama can change my plans.*

"The second semester begins in three weeks." he typed. "There are no changes. All is well." Atta looked at the newspaper headline on his desk. He'd already selected the date. Congress was in session on September 11, 2001. That would insure maximum casualties on Capitol Hill. Kelly Hunter was flying in and out of New York and Boston the whole month of September. Her flight schedule indicated that she would be taking an early morning flight out of Boston, Logan International airport to Los Angeles on September, 11th. This just made it official.

The display remained blank longer than necessary before the hoped for letters spilled across the screen. "He will be pleased." Omar responded. "I will await your confirmation call." As expected, Omar had forgotten about the White House in his excitement over finally setting a date for The Event. Zero Hour.

"Two professors will arrive from the university in two days' time." Omar typed. "Pick them up at Orlando International Airport on August 18th at 3pm." Omar's screen name signed out of the chat room. Atta exited as well.

Relieved, he clicked on the Internet and began printing out airline schedules. The first schedule showed one flight arriving from Dubai on August 18, 2001 at 3pm. He circled it in red ink. *Our last two pilots will be arriving on this one.* he determined. *It is wise to have a replacement if Jarrah backs out.* The next batch of airline schedules was larger. It showed all flights on United, American, and Delta Airlines departing from the East Coast on September 11, 2001. He would book his teams on the selected flights later. For now, he put red dots next to the transcontinental flights that all departed airports near his targets within minutes of each other .

Moving the newspaper aside, Atta picked up a Delta Pilot's Bid package. Kelley Hunter's September flight schedule had been easy enough to get. Her employee number and an automated phone number for her scheduling results were included in the package. *She has chosen to fly from Boston to Los Angeles on a day that Congress is in session.* he thought. He took this as a sign Allah looked with favor on his decision. He'd tweaked the date to match her trip from Boston. Atta put a red arrow pointing to her flight number and felt a shiver of anticipation. Delta flight #1989. *This one was his. He would be the first one to strike at the heart of the Great Santan, making his point even clearer by using the female pilot's aircraft as a missile to take down the North Tower of America's World Trade Center.*

Atta's attention shifted to a disturbing headline on the August 16, 2001 page of the Fort Lauderdale Tribune:

"FBI AGENTS ARREST FLIGHT STUDENT ZACHARIA MOUSSOUI IN MINNESOTA"

It was like watching a train wreck. Atta couldn't look away. Under the sullen photograph of Zacharia Moussaoui was a short blurb.

"An Instructor at the International Flight Academy in Minneapolis contacted the FBI yesterday when he became concerned about the motives of Zacharia

Moussaoui. His behavior led them to believe that they might have a potential hijacker on their hands."

Atta read on, appalled.

"What concerned me most," his simulator instructor told us. "Was that Moussaoui only seemed interested in learning how to climb, descend, and turn an airliner. He didn't want to learn to take off or land them. He was a terrible student."

Mr. Moussaoui, a French National, is being held in jail on immigration charges for overstaying his visa. A federal judge has declined the FBI's request to access Mr. Moussaoui's laptop computer on grounds that it violates his privacy."

A bead of sweat rolled down Atta's forehead and plopped onto the picture of Zacharia Moussaoui. Atta wiped his nose with his sleeve and thought. *Moussaoui's laptop computer has records of all our communications. It has our names, our locations and detailed instructions for 9/11. He's too stupid to cover his tracks.* Atta forced himself to stand up and slow his breathing. He ripped the article out, crumpled it up in a ball and threw it on the floor, as if that would make it go away.

"Marwan!" he shouted. "We must pray. Then we must move everyone again…quickly!"

Chapter Twenty-Nine
Time Is Running Out

August 18, 2001 / 09:35am EST / Holiday Inn Express / Nokomis, Florida

"Airplane travel is nature's way of making you look like your passport photo."

- Vice Presi dent Al Gore

Fletcher had taken an evening flight from DC to Orlando, then driven to the Holiday Inn Express in Nokomis, Florida. It had taken him a few weeks to get the time off and to track down the owner of the house Atta had been renting.

According to the irate landlord, Atta had disappeared three days ago on August 16th, voiding his lease agreement and leaving the owner to figure out how to clean up and pay the bills. The landlord had been eager to let Fletcher in to look at the house this morning. The sooner he could get another renter in to fill the financial gap Atta had left him in, the better.

The nearest Starbucks in Nokomis already had a line of bleary-eyed caffeine addicts. He joined them.

Fletch sat down with his cup and took a bracing sip, reviewing the rest of his plans for the day. A demanding work schedule and the inability to ask his boss for help had been a big problem. Bob backed the NSA's Intelligence Officer in ordering Fletch to stand down where Atta and Kelley were concerned.

I didn't have a choice on that. Fletch told himself. *By all rights this was the National Security Agency's baby and the Air Marshals shouldn't have been privy to the information he'd seen.*

Fletch sighed and drained the last of his coffee. Invigorated, he reached into his pocket and pulled out the flight schedules, bank statements, and a crumpled piece of newspaper he'd found in Atta's trash this morning. He was particularly interested in the flight schedules someone had noted in red marker pen. *Time to get to work.* he told himself. He wondered if his obsession with Atta wasn't just an excuse to stay close to

Kelley. In a way it was, but he also had good reason to suspect Atta of evil intentions on a much larger scale.

Fletcher unfolded the computer print outs of flight schedules and bank statements. The evidence confirmed that Atta's activities were ominous enough to merit his attention. The dog-eared statements from Atta's Sun Trust Bank account indicated that he'd been a busy boy. Atta had booked dozens of flights around the U.S. and Europe for himself and a number of men with Islamic names. Fletch wondered where he got his money from and what he was orchestrating with it.

Atta's bank branch was located in Fort Lauderdale, Florida. On July second, Atta made purchases and cash withdrawals from Boston and Las Vegas. Then Atta ended up back in Fort Lauderdale where he'd started out. *This is standard routine with him.* Fletch noted. Airline tickets, rental cars and photo developing seemed to be Atta's focus.

A week later, Atta had disappeared into Germany and Spain. Now he was apparently back. Fletch needed to know exactly where "back" was. He picked up a second scrap of paper. It was stained with what appeared to be tea and some other substance he'd rather not identify.

The simulator training schedule from a facility outside of Miami had been worth it. Both Atta and Al Shehhi were listed on it. Fletch pulled out his cell phone and dialed the number of the Pan Am Simulator training building in Opa-Locka Florida.

"This is Eugene Fletcher. I have a telephone appointment to speak with the director of your Flight Training department this morning regarding the billing address and any other details he can offer about two of your simulator students, a Mr. Mohammed Atta and a Mr. al Shehhi. I'm verifying job applications they've filed with our company." Yes Mr. Fletcher. I'll see if he's available. Can you hold? Fletcher looked at his watch. It was a long drive from Nokomis to Orlando International Airport. Fletcher wanted to be there in time to see who showed up to meet the passengers on the 3pm Saudi Arabian flight Atta had marked in red ink.

Fletch had chosen not to use his status as a Federal Air Marshal to get information from the Pan Am training facility. He wasn't on a sanctioned mission, and people tended to clam up when you flashed a badge at them. Word also got around when a law enforcement officer asked questions. *That would not be good.* he thought.

"Hello Mr. Fletcher. I'm sorry but the director has been called away for a meeting. Would you like to re-schedule for a call later today?"

Fletch checked his watch. It was time to leave. "No thank you. I can call another day." He swept up his rental car keys and the evidentiary papers, taking his coffee with him. If all went well, he would find far more valuable information at the arrival gates in Orlando International Airport.

* * *

"Are you sure you don't want to make this landing Animal?" Kelley asked. "It's a beautiful day in Orlando and the approach should be a piece of cake."

"I take that as a personal insult." Animal replied, feigning indignation. "You know I get bored if it's too easy."

"Don't you dare take that tobacco out again." Kelley warned, seeing him reach into his pocket. "I've let you spit in that bottle all morning and we have an agreement. No more chewing after three o'clock."

Animal's hand froze in mid-air and he looked at the clock on the 767's instrument panel.

"Yeah. I know. According to the clock it's only 11am." he said defensively.

"It's August 18th local time, not Pacific Daylight time. You're reading the wrong time zone deliberately and you know it." Kelley laughed. "Now step away from the tobacco and put that disgusting bottle somewhere I don't have to look at it."

Animal sighed and did as she asked.

"Hey." Kelley grinned. "Don't look so put-upon. That stuff's bad for you. I don't want my favorite co-pilot getting sick. You need to hang around and keep pestering me."

"That's my purpose in life." he said, pushing the bottle back out of sight. "I keep buddy-bidding with you just to pester you."

"Ah." Kelley replied. "I thought it was because all the other captains run away when they see you coming. You're running out of people to fly with."

"They can't take the competition." Animal said. "You're the only one who makes landings half as good as mine." Animal had been bidding to fly with Kelley ever since she got out of training. He was taking his conversation with the Federal Air Marshal seriously and dutifully sending him copies of Kelley's monthly flight schedule.

I'm getting to be a regular nervous Nellie. he thought in disgust. *I don't even know what I'm supposed to be nervous about.* He resolved to ask Fletcher for a few more details the next time he talked to him. He felt he'd earned that right.

"I see you bid to fly with me in September too." Kelley commented. "There's a great seafood restaurant in Boston. Do you want to go there for dinner on the eleventh? We have a Boston to LA turn-around then."

"Naw. Thanks anyway. I'm flying with my National Guard Wing then." he replied. "It's the only trip I dropped in September. You know how it is. Duty calls."

"O.K." Kelley said. "Be that way. I'll just have to break in another first officer."

"Delta 511 contact Orlando approach on one-three-two decimal two-two" center broke in.

"Looks like we'd better get back to business." Animal said, keying his microphone.

"Yup" Kelley answered, craning her neck to look for the Orlando airport "How about an approach check?"

Chapter Thirty
Near Miss

*August 18, 2001 / 3:15pm EST / Orlando
International Airport / International Customs
arrival / Orlando, Florida*

**"*Close' only counts in horse shoes and hand
grenades."***

-   Anonymous

Fletch stood downstairs at the Orlando
Airport Customs entry point. This time he'd
decided to use his Federal Air Marshal badge
and credentials. *It's worth the risk.* he
thought. All he'd been able to tell the
Customs Inspector and his Supervisor was
that there might be persons of interest
attempting to enter the U.S. on this flight.
They had agreed to cooperate and let him
watch, to the degree that his scant
information allowed.

The wadded-up article on the floor of
Atta's abandoned hotel room and the flight
schedules, particularly this one circled in red
from Dubai, sent up warning flags in

Fletcher's psyche. He'd barely made it back to the airport in time to meet the flight. At this point, he was running on instinct. Not knowing exactly what he was looking for. He did know that he was gathering solid information that might finally implicate Atta in something tangibly sinister. *If all goes well* Fletch calculated, *Atta might show up to meet someone.*

Atta had checked out of the hotel room he'd rented in Orlando last night. Fletch had just missed him. He was finally closing in on the man, and he felt his adrenalin rising.

Mohammed al Qahtani - and Hamid Bin Laden. Atta rolled the names over in his mind as he stood upstairs in the Orlando terminal waiting for the men to arrive. Al Qahtani was fine. Atta did not like the idea that one of Osama's fifty brothers was being sent as a back-up pilot. He felt threatened. *The Bin Laden name alone could cause some confusion as to who is in charge.* he thought. Perhaps Osama had finally seen reason and sent Hamid as a replacement pilot for Ziad Jarrah. Atta relaxed. That would be good news indeed.

The big Saudi Arabian Airlines jet swung into view and taxied toward him. *They will be here soon. I had best prepare.* he told himself. *They will have to go through customs first. Then I will meet them and I will be very clear as to who decides what shall be done.* He crossed his arms and steeled himself for that eventuality.

"They're coming now." the Inspector remarked to the Air Marshal out of the corner of his mouth. Fletch turned to see the doors swing open and a mob of Middle Eastern people sweep through. His heart dropped.

This is hopeless. he realized. *What was I thinking? Other than Atta, I don't even know who I'm looking for.* Fletch remained in his corner scanning faces as they checked through the customs booths and proceeded to the exit doors.

Raised voices and a man angrily waving his arms three booths down caught his attention. The supervisor walked over to see what the commotion was all about.

"I am here for vacation." the man yelled. "A friend is waiting to pick me up! I am Saudi and I have no time for this!" Saudis were usually given special consideration by US customs. Obviously, this man expected his piece of special treatment. His bad attitude determined that he wasn't going to get it.

"I'm sorry Mr. al-Qahtani." the supervisor told him. "You have insufficient money and no credit cards for a long stay here." The Inspector shuffled through his documents.

"You also have no return ticket. We can't allow you into the U.S. under these conditions."

"You will be in very big trouble if you don't!" al Qahtani shouted. "My friend will be upset. I am going through now!" Al Qahtani attempted to shove his way past the Inspectors. A firm hand gripped his arm and he turned to confront the owner. He found himself looking into a pair of predatory deep blue eyes.

"Tell me about the friend who's waiting for you." the man said. The quiet way he said it chilled al-Qahtani."

"There is no friend." he reversed himself. "I have no friend waiting for me." he stated, looking at Fletch defiantly. "I am here by myself."

"You just told us there was a friend waiting." The Inspector objected. "What is his address and phone number?

"You miss-heard me." al-Qahtani countered. "My friend is in Saudi Arabia and you will be held accountable for this affront." he threatened weakly.

The Inspector looked at Fletch, who loosened his grip. There was nothing else he could do.

"As you like Mr. al-Qahtani." the Inspector replied. "The fact remains that you are not entering the United States. We're putting you back on the next flight out to Dubai." He took the man's arm and ushered him into the holding room.

Fletch watched al-Qahtani disappear. He couldn't question him about Atta. Not only was it out of his jurisdiction, but it would get back to Atta if al-Qahtani was involved with him.

* * *

"Thank you, Mr. Bin Laden." the young INS agent said, handing him his passport and papers. "Welcome to America." She glanced in the direction of the commotion at the other end of the room and looked up at the tall smiling Saudi.

"Sorry about that." she nodded in the direction of the conflict as the passenger was led away. "We're usually more hospitable."

"There is no need to apologize." the man replied, grateful for the diversion. "I find your country most welcoming." It was obvious to Bin Laden that al Qahtani was not coming with him. He turned and got on the escalator that would take him upstairs to meet Atta.

Fletch stood outside the customs area with the uneasy feeling that there was something he'd missed. It suddenly hit him. *If Atta's waiting for someone from this flight he might still be upstairs in the gate area.* Fletch waved a hurried thank you to the Customs Inspector and started toward the escalator.

Atta saw the tall Saudi approaching him, but something was wrong. "Where is al-Qahtani?" he demanded.

The man stopped and towered over Atta. Looking over his shoulder he said "Al-Qahtani will not be joining us. He was denied entry in customs. They are sending him back to Dubai."

Atta clenched his fists and asked himself what else could go wrong this day.

"I suggest we leave now." Bin Ladin proclaimed nervously. "There were several men questioning al-Qahtani. This is not a good place for us to be."

The tall man's tone rankled Atta but he realized that Bin Laden's brother was right. "Follow me." Atta ordered "You attract attention with your height." It was the best the five-foot-seven Atta could do to assert his dominance. He was going to make the most of it. The two men moved off down the terminal corridor.

Fletch arrived at the top of the escalator and looked toward the gate area. He searched the crowd for the one face he would recognize. A Delta flight had just finished deplaning at the gate next door. He thought of Kelley every time he saw a Delta jet. It was a curse. *Get your mind back on the business at hand.* Fletch chided himself.

Looking past the Delta gate, he saw the backs of two Middle Eastern men. One noticeably tall and one short and stiff. They disappeared around the corner. Something seemed vaguely familiar about the short one. *What have I got to lose?* Fletch asked himself, starting after them. His path was suddenly blocked by a lantern-jawed man in a Delta pilot's uniform.

"What are you doing here Fletcher?" Animal whispered. "Are you here to see Kelley? Is it O.K. now?" he continued.

Fletcher's mind went into overdrive. He'd been so focused on finding Atta he'd forgotten that Kelley's schedule showed her flying into Orlando this month.

"No." Fletch said. "My orders haven't been lifted. Why? Is she here?" he asked anxiously. His heart desperately wanted to see her but, that would be a disaster.

"Then you'd better hurry up and run because here she comes partner." Animal advised.

Fletch looked and saw a tall flaxen-haired Captain emerging from the jetway door. A group of flight attendants surrounded her. Kelley looked like aviation's version of the Goddess Diana and her nymphs. He couldn't stop looking at her.

"You-had-better-get-out-of-here." Animal repeated. Fletch shook himself and hurriedly moved out of sight.

"Hey!" he heard Animal add as he put distance between them. "I want to know what's going on. Call me."

So do I. Fletch thought as he left them behind. "I'll call you as soon as I figure it out."

Chapter Thirty-One
Last Night on Earth

September 10, 2001 / 10am EST / Washington D.C.

"If you knew you would die tomorrow your soul will be defined by how you choose to spend today."

- Author

"We've already had this conversation, Fletcher. By all rights I should fire you and have you charged with insubordination at the very least!" the voice blasted over the phone. Fletch held it away from his ear. "You disobeyed a direct order!" Bob was angry and Fletch was desperate. It was September 10, 2001. Exasperated breathing on Bob's end of the line continued while he composed himself.

Silence means one of two things. Fletch thought. *Either I've just made the biggest mistake of my life, or Bob's trying to find an acceptable way of helping me.*

"You realize the things you've told me make you sound like a raving lunatic, don't you?" Bob continued. "You can't just go around following a bunch of Saudi's and violating their civil rights on flimsy circumstantial evidence! They haven't done anything wrong."

"Bob." Fletch began. "You know me better than that. I wouldn't have done this if I wasn't certain. I know something very bad's going down tomorrow involving Atta and these men. All of the red flags are there. Kelly Hunter is flying out of Boston tomorrow. We already know Atta's fixated on involving her in whatever he's planning. You wanted to use her as bait because you know he's determined to include her in whatever he's planning involving airliners. " The silence was there again. Fletch didn't know what else to say so he just added "Please."

"It's Robert to you!" the FAM Liaison growled. "Did you know Lt. Colonel Joe Johnson was officially reprimanded last month for trying to follow up on Atta?" Bob said thoughtfully.

"I didn't." Fletch answered. "But it doesn't surprise me." He decided to go for it. *At this point I've got nothing to lose.* he thought. "Did you know" he asked Bob "that I spoke with the FBI Agent on the Moussaoui case and he said he wouldn't be surprised if this character tried to fly an airliner into the World Trade Center?"

"That's ridiculous." Bob sputtered.

"Let me finish." Fletch continued. "The FBI's been trying to get permission to get into Moussaoui's computer but the courts keep denying them access out of concern for his rights to privacy, because he hasn't done anything wrong except overstaying his visa. Are we going to wait until guys like this and Atta kill people before we can take preventative measures or track them? Moussaoui is the man in the news article I found torn out and crumpled up in Atta's hotel room." Fletch took a breath and kept on going. "Another FBI agent in Phoenix has been begging the administration to look into Middle Eastern men in flight schools there doing similar things."

"All coincidental." Bob commented. "Bob." Fletch replied. "We both know terrorist chatter about something big happening in the U.S. has skyrocketed lately. Something IS going to happen. We just don't know what." Evidently Bob was thinking. The telltale tooth-tapping had begun.

"I found flight schedules for September 11th in Atta's trash with Kelly's Delta flight 1989 marked in red." Fletcher added. His desperation clear.

"When I have a difficult decision to make," Bob replied. "I always ask myself what the worst thing that can happen is, if I choose one option or the other. Then I choose the one I'm willing to live with." Fletch held his breath, waiting for the verdict.

"I'm going to give you a month off without pay for insubordination starting tonight." Bob said. Fletch cringed but he knew it could have been worse.

"What I'd suggest you do with this time off is to take a nice vacation." Bob continued. "Why don't you book a flight to Boston tonight. Then book the early morning flight on Delta tomorrow to Los Angeles? I believe Delta Flight #1989 to Los Angeles would be an excellent choice."

"I can do that." was all Fletch could think of to say. Bob knew Flight #1989 was Kelley's flight. It was also the one Atta had marked with a red arrow.

"I can live with the consequences of that decision." Bob replied. "If you're wrong or if you're right, I think you can too."

"I can live with the consequences." Fletch agreed.

"If you're right" Bob continued. "I'll reinstate your pay for the month." Bob took a minute to think about what he'd said. "Hell." he decided in a fit of generosity. "If you're right I'll double it."

"Thank you." Fletch replied, emotionally exhausted. "Have a nice trip." Bob replied. "Try to stay alive." A dial tone signaled the end of the conversation.

Fletch looked at the phone in his hand for a moment, then hung up and selected a well-worn number. "Hello Angela. Can I speak with the kids please?" He waited for his ex-wife to finish asking him what he wanted.

"Nothing special." he said. "Yes. I'm aware that my next visitation isn't for two weeks. I just want to tell them I love them."

* * *

"I love you too kiddo." Kelley called after the blur of her son as he scooted out the door. "Drive safe and have fun." she added. It took a conscious effort on her part not to badger him with other motherly advice like "Make sure you eat enough." He'd be staying with friends for a few days anyway.

"See ya' later mom. Have a nice trip." The slamming of the door punctuated his departure.

Kelly smiled at the thought of her son of the boundless energy and turned to the batch of bills waiting for her on the table. She looked at them and the clock on the counter. *I'll do the bills after I get home from sparring.* she decided. Feeling like she was playing hooky, she ran upstairs to change. *It took another martial artist to understand how a bunch of apparently sane people could have so much fun beating each other up.*

Kelley trotted down the basement stairs to get her sparring gear. On the way, she swept up the bow and arrow that hung by her home dojo's door. She drew the arrow back to the corner of her mouth and released it. The shaft sizzled through the hallway and into a target on the far wall of the basement storage room. A solid "thunk" announced its arrival as it buried its point in the large red bull's-eye.

"Got-cha!" Kelley announced, putting the bow back and slinging her bag over her shoulder. She slowed on her way up the stairs and looked back at the target. An image of passionate blue eyes under sweeping dark brows teased at her heart. She'd adopted Fletcher's method for stress relief. It allowed her to keep a little of him with her.

"Take care you wherever you are Fletcher." she whispered.

***

Atta was livid. The blood pounding in his temples made his head feel like it was about to explode. He was living his worst nightmare.

"It is not your decision to make." Hamid Bin Laden smiled down at him. "I have been well trained to find and destroy the White House, and I have experience flying the 767 simulator. I do not need to explain myself or Osama's Fatwa's to YOU." Hamid Bin Laden had just informed Atta that Delta Flight #1989 was the 5th plane that Osama bin Laden had earmarked for the White House.

Atta would not be flying it. Hamid would. Atta was going to fly American Airlines flight 11 into the North Tower of the World Trade center as planned, instead of Delta 1989. Hamid held up the large Delta Airlines pilot uniform. "You would look like a mouse lost in a tent in this." he laughed.

It was the morning of September 10th, and they had waited until now to tell Atta of this change of plans? Atta was furious.

Looking at Atta, Marwan feared he was having a heart attack. His face was red and spittle frothed the corners of his mouth. Atta's whole body shook with rage and shame.

Hamid Bin Laden continued to smile benevolently at the fuming Atta.

"You have betrayed me!" Atta shouted, lunging toward Bin Laden in an uncharacteristic display of emotion. Marwan was shocked. Atta looked like a terrier attacking a Great Dane.

Bin Laden's brother didn't seem surprised. He just grabbed Atta, hoisted him off the floor and laughed as Atta kicked and swung at him in desperate futility.

Marwan averted his eyes. Hamid flipped Atta around and slammed him face down on the bed, twisting his arm behind him and placing a knee in the small of his back. "You must learn humility before it is too late Mohammed." Hamid spoke calmly. "Your place in this great holy event is to fly the American jet into the North Tower of the

World Trade Center, as planned. İt is not yours to dictate what will be."

Atta was horrified. He felt his eyes watering in mortification as he struggled against the rough blankets pressing against his face. He couldn't breathe. He couldn't move. He could hear Marwan beginning to sing one of his Jihad songs glorifying Islamic martyrdom and could picture him dancing to it as he often did. Atta knew it was his way of trying to calm himself, but it suddenly created a different picture all together in Atta's fevered mind. *I am surrounded by madmen!* he thought desperately.

"Will you calm yourself now Mohammed, or must I send you back to Afghanistan for rest and use another pilot?" Bin Laden asked. Atta stopped moving and tried to speak into the blanket. Hamid allowed him to get up. "What was that you said?" he asked sternly.

Atta swallowed and kept his eyes down. "I asked your forgiveness and said that it will be as you say brother." He glanced up at the corner of the room where Ziad Jarrah stood, and saw him smile. Atta's calculating mindset returned and forced his anger back.

"It is done then." Hamid said. "We will pray together this morning and catch our flights to position ourselves tonight." Atta stood and listened to Osama bin Laden's brother rearrange his plans. "Mohamed el-Amir Atta." he repeated. "Your American flight 11 will attack the North Tower of the World Trade Center." he turned to Al Shehhi. "Marwan. You will take United Flight 175 into the South Tower. I will take Delta flight 1989 to destroy the White House."

Atta looked at Marwan who continued to dance and sing in his self-induced trance. *He looks like a puppet on strings.* Atta thought unkindly.

Hamid droned on with the preparation for the martyrs "Shave the extra hair on your body. Perfume and ritually wash yourself, purify yourself so that you will be acceptable in the eyes of Allah." The others listened in mesmerized fascination. "Check your knives, tools and identity papers. Keep your clothing tight about you and keep reciting the sacred phrases."

He looked directly at Atta. "Remind yourself to listen and obey this night. Obey Allah and his messenger, and do not quarrel."

Atta lowered his gaze. Hamid took the gesture as submission. He didn't see the flat black pupils expanding to the cold dead eyes of a shark. "*You will be leaving from Boston tomorrow and so will I.* Atta thought. *Things change.* The men knelt and prayed for a successful slaughter. Then they left for various hotel rooms in Washington, New Jersey, Boston and Portland, Maine.

Atta and one of his more attractive henchmen, Abdul Aziz al-Omari got in a rental car and drove to Portland Maine that evening. The two of them spent their evening shopping at Wal-Mart and eating at Pizza Hut. The next morning, they would argue about a parking space at the airport. They would almost miss their flight.

Several of the Saudi men in Boston made a series of telephone calls trying to arrange for prostitutes on the last night. In the end they thought the prices were too high and didn't employ anyone.

Ziad Jarrah spent his last night on earth at a Day's Inn in Newark New Jersey. He wrote one last letter to his wife, Aysel. For once he didn't lie to her. "Hello my dear Aysel, my love, my life. You should be very proud of me. What I am going to do is an honor and you will see the results and everybody will be happy...."

Chapter Thirty-Two
9/11 Unholy War

September 11, 2001 / 07:30 – 08:15am EST /
New York JFK / Boston Logan / Washington
Dulles International Airports

"-Let's Roll"

-   Todd Beamer, Passenger United
Flight 93

Something slammed into the back of his seat, causing him to slosh a wave of orange juice onto half of his neatly starched shirt. "What the...?" Captain Granger sputtered and juggled the rest of the liquid in his cup. The two men who stormed into his cockpit hitting his headrest and making demands didn't seem to notice or care.

"We must take off NOW!" the one named Ahmed instructed. "We are five minutes late. We cannot be late!" he blustered at the captain.

"We cannot be late!" the other Saudi repeated, pointing anxiously at his watch. "We must leave NOW."

"Gentlemen." Captain Granger replied, scrubbing at his shirt with a napkin. "ATC has issued a ground stop for all aircraft right now. I've already announced that. We aren't leaving until ATC lets us leave. For all I know, it could take another hour. Now please, go take your seats."

"No!" Ahmed replied. "We will not take our seats until you agree to go NOW." The men stood threateningly behind his chair.

"Well then gentlemen," Captain Granger stated, getting out of his seat and forcing them out of his space. "This is how it's going to be. Get off my airplane." He kept advancing until they were outside of the cockpit.

Turning to the gate agent he said "Jim, would you please make an announcement and tell all of the passengers to wait in the gate area?" He looked meaningfully at Ahmed and his four companions. "Particularly these fellows. With a police escort if necessary. " he instructed.

"Yes captain." Jim said, looking at the Saudis. "Are you going to require a police escort?" he asked them politely.

"No." Ahmed replied sullenly as they gathered their bags. Captain Granger walked back into the cockpit wiping at his shirt with a wet rag.

"Wow." the first officer said. "I didn't know you were such a hard-ass."

"About eight months ago on my first flight as captain, it took Kelly Hunter and some nasty weather to teach me that my job is to say no and piss people off."

An hour later the Twin Towers, the Pentagon and a field in Pennsylvania would be in flames. The Islamic men waiting for Captain Granger's flight in the gate area had disappeared. His passengers, crew and 30,000 people living around three of America's biggest nuclear power plants would live to see September 12th.

* * *

Fletch inched his way toward the security gate at Boston's Logan International Airport. The line snaked along forever.

Today I'm just another passenger. he thought. *I have no authority, no firearm, and no special FAM privileges.* Bob's disciplinary action required Fletch to leave his gun and credentials behind. Fletcher still carried two of his favorite knives and his FAM badge concealed inside his jacket in direct violation of Bob's orders, just in case. *Half the time knives don't even set off the TSA alarms. When they do anything 3 inches long or less are legal for passengers to carry with them on airliners.* Fletch wondered how many inches of blade the bureaucrat who wrote the regulation thought it took to kill a person.

He walked through the TSA machine unchallenged and picked up his coat on the other side.

"Sir, would you step over here?" A teenager in a security uniform and a Mohawk squawked the request in his best pubescent voice. He motioned Fletch aside.

"Is something wrong?" Fletch asked.

"Nope. I just have to pick a passenger for a random check." he explained, indicating that Fletcher should raise his arms and turn around.

"Could you hurry it up please." Fletch said checking the time. "I don't want to miss my plane".

"Everybody's in a hurry." the kid replied, wondering what was causing his wand to beep. "Take off your belt."

At Newark, Boston, and Washington Dulles International Airports nineteen other men were walking through security check points, just like Fletch was. They were armed with pepper spray, utility knives and box cutters. All the men made it successfully through security without being stopped. The others were already on board.

Hamid Bin Laden sat at the gate in his Delta pilot uniform waiting to board Flight #1989 as a jump seat rider. From his vantage point he could look into the cockpit and see a blonde female in the captain's seat and a red headed youth in the co-pilot's seat.

Abomination! he thought, his eyes narrowing. It was the one thing he and Atta agreed on. Hamid looked at his watch and reviewed his strategy. *I will ride in the cockpit jump seat and cut the throats of the female and her co-pilot when the seat belt sign is turned off at 10,000 feet.* Hamid went through a last review of their coordinated plans. *Then Jamal will join me to keep the others out of the cockpit while I turn the 767 toward the White House.*

All the hijacked planes had to be taken over within the same fifteen-minute time-period. After that, the military would realize what they were doing and shoot them down. The seat belt sign was routinely turned off when airliners reached 10,000 feet. It was the perfect cue to begin their choreographed massacres.

Hamid wasn't worried about interference from the cabin crew or passengers. The three remaining terrorists in coach and first-class would kill at least two of the most defenseless looking people immediately. That would intimidate the rest. He smiled at the thought. Anyone watching him only saw a tall dark Delta pilot in a good mood.

In another part of the terminal, Atta and Al-Omari were getting off their commuter flight from Portland Maine to Boston and walking into the concourse. "I told you we would not have to go through security again." Atta reassured his companion. The two were dressed in cheap Wal Mart golf shirts and dockers. They looked as non-threatening as any of the other passengers.

Atta looked down the concourse toward the Delta gates. He fingered the other ticket for American flight #11 in his pocket. Atta had purchased it for Hamid Bin Laden. He intended to pressure Hamid into accepting the idea that plans had changed at the last minute, and that they were to switch planes again. It was too late for Hamid to check or verify anything now. *I can hijack the aircraft from first class almost as easily as Hamid can from the cockpit.* He thought. *Our strategy remains the same.*

"Go ahead and board the American flight Abdul." he instructed. "I will join you shortly." The young terrorist looked at Atta with his big doe eyes and started toward Flight #11.

Atta checked the digital time display on the wall and started a brisk walk toward the

Delta gates. He came around the corner in time to see the last of Flight 1989's hijacking team boarding the Delta 767. Hamid Bin Laden was standing at the podium being issued a pilot's jump seat pass.

Quickening his pace, Atta almost collided with another passenger who seemed to be in an equal hurry. The man had just sprinted off the escalator. Atta looked up irritably, and skidded to a stop.

Looking back at him were a pair of deep blue hunter's eyes. The shock in them dissipated and the dark winged brows drew down in recognition. The last time Atta had seen that look was over the barrel of a gun. His mind went into high gear, weighing the odds. He skittered around the man and continued walking rapidly toward Hamid Bin Laden.

Fletch had expected to find Atta. He didn't expect to do it by literally running over him. He started to follow the suspected terrorist. What he saw next made him hesitate. The tall Delta pilot with Middle Eastern features bent down and spoke to Atta.

"Mohammed. What are you doing here?" Bin Laden asked, looking at the little man and hoping he wasn't deranged enough to risk a confrontation.

"I came to wish you luck brother, and to tell you that you are more deserving of this flight than I." Atta locked eyes with Fletch and grabbed the tall Saudi in a traditional Islamic greeting. He kissed him three times on his cheeks, the traditional Al Qaeda greeting, and loudly said "Inshallah. I wish you luck. I love you all." while looking over Hamid's shoulder, directly into the eyes of Fletch. Atta's bloodless lips stretched into a triumphant smirk. Releasing Hamid, Atta walked back to his fate aboard American Airlines Flight #11.

Hamid Bin Laden looked around furtively. Then he turned and walked onto the Delta Flight. Fletch could see him entering the cockpit through the terminal window. Then he looked at Atta's tiny figure as it disappeared in the other direction. Risking one last desperate look at Kelly and the tall jump seat rider positioning himself behind her, Fletch turned and sprinted after Atta.

Chapter Thirty-Three
No Turning Back

September 11, 2001 / 07:55am EST / Boston Logan International Airport / Delta Airlines flight #1989

"What we anticipate seldom occurs. What we least expected generally happens."

-   Benjamin Disraeli

"We've only got thirty-one passengers today, Kelly." Shaheera said, handing her the final paperwork. "That's not counting one no-show. We're going to close the doors early if that's OK with you."

"Thanks." Kelly said, taking the papers and glancing at the cargo door lights. "The cargo doors are just closing. You can close the cabin door now. I'll tell the tug we're ready to push back."

Shaheera looked at the tall man wedged into the jump seat behind Kelly. "You look cramped in there." she said amiably. "We have plenty of seats available in First Class if you'd rather sit back here."

Any jump seater will jump at that upgrade offer. Kelly thought, fully expecting him to leave.

"No." Hamid replied. "It is a big cockpit. I will stay here to observe for training."

Shaheera shrugged and went back to tend the people in her first-class section.

"Oh." the young co-pilot stated. "Are you on a familiarization flight then?"

"Yes."

"What equipment are you training on?" Kelly asked absently, just to be sociable.

"This kind." he replied.

Kelly glanced away from her work and raised a questioning eyebrow at her red-headed first officer. He shrugged as if to say "I don't know what his problem is either."

"Hamid Bin Laden." Kelly searched her memory for the reason that name sounded familiar, and decided she must have seen it on the seniority list. *He certainly won't win any personality contests.* she thought. Kelley felt his knees jab into the back of her seat as

he loomed over her headrest. He made her feel uncomfortable in more ways than one.

"We're closing the doors now." Shaheera informed her. "See you in the air."

"See you soon." Kelley replied, reaching up and turning on the fasten seat belt sign.

The cockpit door slammed shut. She heard the passenger entry door thud shut as well. Kelley picked the microphone up to request clearance to push back from the gate. The image of American Airlines Flight 11 lifting off the runway was reflected in the terminal window. She glanced idly at it, thinking it looked pretty against the sunrise.

"Captain." the voice of the tug driver crackled through her head set. "The cargo's loaded, but the agent says we have to let a last-minute passenger on."

"O.K." Kelley sighed. "I'll call the flight attendants and tell them to open the door again. As soon as the passenger is on board and seated, we'll push back."

Shaheera disarmed the emergency exit slide and rotated the handle, pulling the heavy door open. Fetcher's sweating face appeared in front of her. *He'd changed his mind halfway down the concourse and decided on a choice he could live with.* Fletch was breathing hard as he pressed a piece of paper into her hand.

Shaheera's jaw dropped and her brow wrinkled in surprise. She gathered her wits to tell the man off. *He'd hurt her friend and she wasn't going to let him get away with it.*

Fletch shook his head "no" and made a head tilt and eye roll toward the passengers. His eyes begged her to remain silent. She fixed him with a scathing look as he went to sit down in the farthest aisle seat of First class.

Girl. You always were a sucker for a beautiful man. Shaheera thought, shutting the cabin door again. The aircraft pushed back and taxied toward Runway 4R as the flight attendants picked up cups and glasses, making sure seat belts were fastened and tray tables were stowed. When Shaheera made the required list of announcements she refused to grant Fletch the courtesy of looking at him.

"Ladies and gentlemen." Kelly's voice announced over the P.A. "We've just been cleared onto the runway. We'd like to ask our flight attendants to please be seated for takeoff." Shaheera secured herself in one of the Flight attendant jump seats that were facing forward, attached to the bulkhead between the galley and the first-class section.

If I wasn't facing forward right now, Shaheera thought *I'd glare holes right through him! How dare he get on Kelly's flight? What does he think he's doing poking notes at me?* She huffed at the audacity. The 767 accelerated down the runway, G-forces pushing Shaheera back into her seat as it rotated. Delta flight 1989 lifted off with a comforting roar and rolled left to intercept its' departure course to Los Angeles.

Shaheera's curiosity finally got the better of her. She reached into her apron pocket and took out the note Fletch had pressed into her hand. Unfolding it, she fully expected a plea for her to intervene with Kelley on his behalf. *No way mister!* she thought. *You blew it!*

Her expression froze as she read the brief words hastily scrawled on the paper.

"I am a Federal Air Marshall. Please do not indicate my position on this aircraft to anyone. I suspect the man sitting in Captain Hunter's jump seat is not a Delta pilot. He is a suspected terrorist intent on hijacking this aircraft. There are probably others with him sitting in the cabin."

Her hand shook as she read the final words.

"Please pass this note to Captain Hunter immediately, without alerting the man in the jump seat behind her."

How in God's name am I supposed to do that? She wondered. Shaheera loosened her shoulder harnesses and peeked around the bulkhead at Fletch. He'd been waiting for her to acknowledge him. When he saw her frightened eyes seeking his, he knew she'd read his note.

Fletch looked at the dark heads of the two Middle Eastern men a few seats in front of him. They were bent to some task. All his training told him these were at least two of the accomplices. He didn't know if, or how many more might be in coach. The only other people in first class were a distinguished elderly couple sitting three rows ahead of him.

Shaheera saw Fletcher raise a warning finger to his lips and point at the two men sitting in front of him. She nodded and sat back behind her wall. Looking at the thin blonde flight attendant sitting next to her, Shaheera made a snap decision. *Dawn's a new hire, but she needs to know this too.* She tapped her on the shoulder, held a finger to her lips and handed her the note.

The girl smiled at her and opened it like a teenager at a slumber party, expecting gossip. Her big blue eyes widened in alarm. She looked at Shaheera and inhaled.

This was a mistake! Shaheera realized in horror. *It's going to be one whopping big scream.*

Shaheera drew her hand back and slapped the blonde smartly on the cheek, startling her back to her senses. Then she clapped a hand over the flight attendant's mouth. Tears welled in the big blue eyes but she nodded, indicating she wouldn't scream.

Shaheera hugged her and whispered "It will be O.K. Dawn You just have to keep calm. I'm going up with the note for Kelley."

"What seat is the Air Marshall in?" Dawn asked hopefully.

"4C." Shaheera said, as a pacifier. "Don't look."

In the cockpit, the altimeter indicated they were approaching ten thousand feet. The altitude where the fasten seat belt sign would be turned off. The flight attendant call bell rang. Kelly switched to the interphone. "Cockpit." she answered.

"Captain, I have something for you, and I must come to the cockpit immediately. Shaheera answered using the crew code language for "Hijacking."

Puzzled at the cryptic message and the stress in Shaheera's voice, Kelly hit the "unlock" button for the cockpit door and said "Come on up. Door's open."

"Hey. That's a pretty neat tool you've got there." the first officer commented as he watched Bin Laden open a multi-purpose tool. "We're not allowed to do maintenance on these airplanes." he kidded.

"I don't intend to do maintenance." Hamid replied, transferring the tool to his other hand and out of sight. He thumbed the blade open and concealed it under his thigh. *Rejoice in death.* he reminded himself.

A strange transmission from another aircraft crackled over the cockpit speakers.

"We have some airplanes. Everybody stay in your seats! Don't do anything stupid. This is the captain. We are going back to the airport to land." Someone screamed in the background. Atta was in the captain's seat of American Flight #11. The pilots were dead and Atta had made a mistake. He'd flipped the wrong switch and was transmitting to Air Traffic Control and all the other aircraft on frequency, instead of his passengers.

Kelley and her co-pilot looked at each other in confusion. "Did you hear that?" the First officer asked. "What the Hell was that?"

Chapter Thirty-Four
Living by The Sword

September 11, 2001 / 08:15 EST / DAL flight #1989

"Do unto others as you would have them do unto you."

-   The Bible and The Qur'an

The cockpit door opened, interrupting the disturbing radio transmission. Shaheera came in with a pot of hot coffee. "Coffee anyone?" she asked cheerfully, balancing the pot in one hand and a piece of folded paper in the other.

Before they could answer, Shaheera bent down to Kelley and shoved the note into her hand. "I'd REALLY suggest you open it IMMEDIATELY." She looked at Kelley and then back at the note as if forcing her to open it by sheer willpower. Kelley had never seen Shaheera act like this. She wondered what was wrong with her. Kelley took the note and unfolded it.

Thirty seconds later the first officer flipped the seat belt sign off. "I'll get that for you captain." he said, giving her time to read. Shaheera stood up and deliberately stumbled against Hamid. Hot coffee poured out of the pot and into his lap. Hamid cursed as it landed, searing his most sensitive parts. He released his seat belt, stood up, and hit Shaheera in the face, knocking her out the partially open cockpit door.

Fletch saw Shaheera fly out of the cockpit. She hit the galley wall just before Hamid yanked the door closed again. Shaheera slumped to the floor, unconscious.

The two Islamic men in the seats ahead of Fletch had tied red bandannas around their heads. They stood up shouting "Stay seated! We have the airplane! We have a bomb!" The men brandished knives and box cutters in their hands. One grabbed the delicate looking elderly woman by the hair and jerked her to her feet, backhanding the older man when he tried to intervene.

The slender blonde flight attendant lost it. "Oh my God they're getting up!" she screamed, making a bee line for Fletcher.

"They're getting up! They're getting up!" Dawn continued running toward Fletcher demanding he do something. He tried to look harmless, appalled at what she was doing. It was no use. His cover was blown. The two men turned and looked at him, appraising the threat. Fletch did the only thing he could do. He stood up and screamed in his highest falsetto voice, "Oh my God they're getting uupp!" Flapping his hands in distress against his cheeks, Fletch did his best impression of a flaming Queen.

Dawn and the two terrorists all stopped and looked at him. The one holding the elderly woman dropped her and stepped toward noisier, more easily subdued prey. The other grabbed Dawn by the hair and pulled her head back.

Fletch feigned trying to hide behind the seat back as he bent and drew the knife out of its sheath in his boot.

"Allahu Akbar!" the man yelled, grabbing for Fletcher's shirt and lunging with the knife on his multi-tool.

Fletch parried his hand aside and bent it forward in a submission grip, bringing the man close and forcing the knife into the terrorist's abdomen. "You're right." he grunted. "God is good. You are not." He continued the move upward in a deer gutting motion. Then he swept it out and across the man's throat to finish the job. Fletch knew this fight would be to the death.

He shoved the dying man out of the way and looked at the other terrorist. The man couldn't seem to make up his mind whether to slit Dawn's throat, or go for the pepper spray in his seat.

"I have a bomb!" a voice from behind the curtains in coach screamed. "Stay seated! I have a bomb!" Other screams from the cabin joined him.

In the cockpit, Kelly had hit her seat belt release as soon as Hamid jumped up and slammed the door closed. His distraction had been momentary. Hamid's arm moved in a swinging motion at the edge of her vision, toward the young co-pilot. She heard screaming from the cabin.

"Get out!" Kelly yelled at Hamid, horrified at the startled expression on her co-pilot's face as Hamid's knife ripped through the left side of his neck in a fountain of blood. It spattered Kelley and the bulk of the control panel in a slippery hot blanket. Kelly swiveled her attention to see Hamid reaching for her, his knife on the backswing.

Just like killing the dogs we practice on in Afghanistan. Hamid thought. His mind filled with blood lust.

The co-pilot's leg kicked in a death spasm, hitting the rudder pedal. The big jet lurched to the left, tossing Bin Laden off balance. As Kelley adapted to the surreal situation, her mind and body clicked into the mode she'd practiced all her life. Her co-pilot had bought her the time she needed to flip the mental switch to fight mode.

Hamid Bin Laden's knife seemed to sweep by her in slow motion as he slipped on the co-pilot's blood. She dodged the arc and parried his arm. Outraged anger and fear cooled to ice cold instinct. Kelley's drive to protect and survive released the killer inside.

Everyone has a red-button trigger point. Kelley had found hers.

Hamid stumbled to his knees behind her and grabbed her seat back for support, attempting to pull himself up as he swung the knife again. Half standing in her seat, Kelly turned toward Hamid and braced her knees against the armrests. She slapped the knife edges of her hands together on either side of Hamid's wrists, hitting the nerves that forced his hand open. The weapon flew out and clattered to the floor, wedged between the throttle pedestal and her seat. Kelly's right hand shot out like a cobra, striking Hamid hard in the throat with stiffened fingers.

Hamid didn't have time to worry about not being able to breathe, much less what had happened to his knife. The last thing he saw was another blur of Kelley's hands. The pain was excruciating as her thumbs dug into his eyes.

She fought past the gag factor and secured her grip by grabbing his ears and pushing her thumbs deeper. He screamed through his swelling windpipe and fought to push her away. His fist hit her temple, her cheek, anything he could make contact with. His other hand grabbed her hair, yanking her toward him. Kelley went with it. Pushing off her seat, she catapulted over the backrest and landed on top of Hamid.

He clawed and kicked, knocking the wind out of her. All of Kelly's weight went into her thumbs when she hit. She felt a sickening "pop" as his eyes gave way. Hamid could barely scream through his swollen larynx. He lost interest in anything but his pain, writhing on the cockpit floor in agony, clutching at his ruined eyes and struggling to breathe.

Kelley scrambled as far away from him as she could get, trying to wipe the gore from her hands, and looking for something to hit him with. She'd have to step over the flailing Hamid to get to the crash ax. The 767's autopilot was still on. It began righting itself from the co-pilot's last struggles. Someone was trying to beat down the cockpit door. They were screaming for Hamid to let them in.

Fletch and Jamal found themselves glaring at each other in a standoff. Both had just picked themselves up from the Dutch roll whipsawing of the jet. Fletch was holding his bloody knife, and someone was yelling threats about blowing up the airplane behind a curtain only two feet away. Jamal held a knife and a screaming flight attendant while listening to the crashes in the cockpit. His leader's voice was punctuating the din with hoarse screams.

Dawn broke the tie by fainting, dead weight in Jamal's grip. He dropped her, grabbed the pepper spray and started ramming the cockpit door with his shoulder, yelling for Hamid to open it. Something was not going well in the cockpit. He had to get in.

Fletch turned to the immediate threat. He pulled the curtain aside enough to see the back of the would-be bomber just inches away. One flight attendant was lying dead or injured in the aisle. Another stood facing the bomber, small but fierce, defiantly putting herself between the bomber and her terrified passengers.

The man with what appeared to be explosives wrapped around him seemed to be the only hijacker in the aft cabin. He was facing the passengers in the economy section. Keeping them out of first class. Fletch glanced over his shoulder to make sure Jamal was still preoccupied with the cockpit door.

Satisfied that he was, at least for another few seconds, Fletcher turned back toward the bomber and balanced on the balls of his feet. Positioning the knife in his hand, he drew back the curtain. This had to be done quickly, perfectly, or they would all die. The man was holding a dead man's trigger in his upraised hand. If it was a real bomb, it would detonate the moment he released the trigger. Fletch grabbed the man's hand in a vice-like grip. His right hand jammed his knife into the notch at the base of the man's skull, severing his spinal column. The terrorist crumpled to the floor. The passengers screamed, not knowing if this was a good thing or a bad thing gone worse. Fletcher knew the man was paralyzed from the neck down. *If he isn't dead, he'll never move again.* he thought. Fletch called to the stunned flight attendant in coach. "I need your help! I'm a Federal Air Marshal. Give me your hands!"

She came forward, finding hope in finally having a job to do. "What's your name?" Fletcher asked. It was a quick way to build trust, bond and form a team. "Gaylynn." she said. "Tell me what to do."

"I'm Federal Air Marshal Fletcher. Call me Fletch." He placed her hands firmly over his own. "This is a dead-man's switch he's gripping. You'll be fine as long as you don't let go of his hand. The pressure of his thumb is keeping this switch deactivated. Don't let go. Understand? She nodded and helped Fletch transfer the switch to her hands. "I have to get to the cockpit." he said. "Don't let go." She nodded more confidently. He could see the determination in her eyes. He nodded back.

Fletch turned to see the cockpit door fly open as Jamal broke through the door latch. Jamal raised the can of pepper spray in one hand. His knife was ready in the other.

It was a slaughterhouse inside the cockpit. Kelly looked like a piece of bloody meat. The co-pilot lay slumped sideways over the control pedestal. It was obvious he was dead. Fletch knew he'd never make it to the cockpit in time to stop Jamal.

Kelly barely had time to move out of the way before the door caved in. A wild-eyed man with a red bandanna tied around his head looked down at the writhing Hamid Bin Laden. Then he looked at her and pointed a can of pepper spray. Murder in his eyes. His knife would be next.

Shaheera's angry face rose up behind him as she swung, two-handed. A resounding clang announced the connection of a fire extinguisher with Jamal's skull. He fell sideways into the galley, going with the momentum of the impact. Kelley and Shaheera looked at each other over his body. A large lump offset the perfection of Shaheera's cheek. Her lip was swollen and cut. Kelly looked just plain terrifying.

Peering past Shaheera, Kelley saw Fletcher standing in the aisle amid several dead hijackers and a dozen weeping passengers. He was covered in blood. His hair in wild disarray and his clothing torn. He was bleeding through his shirt from an injury to his rib cage. Kelley blinked and slumped against the doorjamb.

"What are you doing here?" she asked stupidly.

He moved a shoulder as if it hurt and risked taking his eyes from the cabin. "Keeping my promise," he stated. "I came back for you."

Her world went into focus again. Kelley realized she'd been going into shock. Now she could hear the radio chatter and the hoarse wheezing gasps of Hamid. She said the first thing that came into her mind "Are you all right ?"

"I need to make a sweep of the cabin." he said. " I think we got them all. Are you O.K.?"

She looked at her dead co-pilot and the equally horrifying sight of the man she'd mutilated on the floor. "I have to be for now." she said. "I'm the only pilot we've got." Kelly raised her eyes and filled them with Fletch. It was the only way she could cleanse her mind of the carnage around her. His body was poised for action and he exuded the sense that nothing mattered to him but her. They both knew what they had to do.

"How many bad guys up front Kelly? Dead or injured?" he scanned the cabin behind him warily. "How many of us?" Everyone in the aft cabin seemed frozen in time. Watching and wondering what was next. Small desperate whimpers wafted around them like the ghosts of happier times.

The taste of copper and salt invaded her senses as she licked her chapped lips. Kelly tried to push back the knowledge that it was blood, and the thought of whose blood it might be. Rage and a crippling guilt pushed at the edges of her consciousness. She forced them both down.

"My First Officer's dead." she stated bitterly. "We've got one attacker up here. The big man in a pilot uniform. He's temporarily out of commission in the cockpit and another one is unconscious in the galley." What little adrenalin she had left spiked when she saw Dawn on the floor.

"Fainted but fine." Fletch assured her. He looked at the man with the bomb lying face down on the floor in the cabin and the crumpled form of the first terrorist at his feet. "These other two Tangos' aren't getting up again." His face echoed that sentiment before he turned and stalked through the aft cabin, hunting any remaining threats.

Kelly glanced appraisingly over the rest of the cabin and saw the silver haired couple cringing against the bulkhead. The man was holding his wife and stroking her hair as she sobbed softly into his chest. "You're going to be all right now folks." she promised. "You're in good hands. We're going to land at the closest suitable airport." The man nodded, wide eyed, over the soft silver strands of his wife's hair.

Kelly's smile conveyed more reassurance than she felt as she turned back to her grim duties in the cockpit. Picking up a blanket, Kelly laid it gently over the sad remains of her first officer. She looked at Hamid, wanting to finish the job. She could almost feel the gratifying crunch as she imagined breaking his neck.

"Shaheera, get this S.O.B. out of my cockpit and secure both of these guys with duct tape, zip ties, belts. Whatever we've got. Can you help me?" Shaheera nodded, looking at the writhing screaming mess on the floor that was Osama bin Laden's brother."

"Can I knock him out with my fire extinguisher first? Be my guest." Kelley said. "I couldn't get to the crash ax in time." Shaheera sobbed out a few angry hiccupping giggles, then composed herself and picked up the fire extinguisher. Kelley stepped out of the way to give her room to swing. Shaheera came in. Another resounding clang announced that Hamid had been tranquillized. Grabbing the crash ax off the bulkhead, Kelley smiled grimly, set the ax between her flight kit and her chair, and secured herself in the left seat.

She looked out the window. "Shaheera. Get someone to help you drag this guy out of the cockpit immediately. Maybe the older gentleman in first-class can help you. I've got to land this plane." Shaheera leaned over and peered out. An F-16 fighter was flying close formation outside.

"Delta Airlines Flight 1989, please switch frequency to 121.5 and verify you are still in command of the aircraft or you will be shot down." the clipped voice instructed. "This is your last warning." The cockpit speaker went ominously silent.

Kelley fumbled to get her headset on and switch frequencies. "Aircraft flying off my wing, this is Captain Kelley Hunter, captain of Delta flight #1989 and I am in control of my aircraft. Repeat. I am in control of Delta flight #1989. Do NOT fire on this aircraft." The silence was deafening as the fighter pilot scrutinized them.

"Shaheera." Kelly said, not taking her eyes off the fighter pilot. "I know this is hard, but you've got to drag this guy out of my cockpit and secure both of these hijackers immediately. If one of them gets up, we're done. These fighters are going to assume we're still in the hands of terrorists and they'll shoot us down. I'll handle this part". She reassured Shaheera. "Just get him out of my cockpit."

Shaheera squeezed Kelley's shoulder and left.

"Delta. There appear to be several dead or injured people and blood in your cockpit. You don't look much like an airline pilot. Can you verify who you are?"

At least he hears me. Kelley thought desperately. *He hasn't dropped back into firing position yet. How am I supposed to prove I am who I am?"* Kelly estimated she only had a three-minute window to figure it out before the fighters did what they had to do. She looked out again. The fighter had vanished. *So much for that option.* she thought, swallowing hard. Her thumb hovered over the autopilot disconnect button. She knew she couldn't dodge a missile, but she was going to try.

Another F-15 rose up beside her in place of the one who left. The visored helmet turned in her direction. "Delta Flight #1989 this is the wingman from Squadron 102. Am I looking at Captain Kelley Hunter?"

She looked at the figure and keyed her microphone.

"Yes." she rasped dryly, licking her lips. "This is Delta Airlines Captain Kelly Hunter and I have control of my aircraft."

"This is Animal, and you look like shit. Tell me what you won't let me do after three O'clock if you're in full command of the aircraft, and we'll escort you down to Cleveland for a landing."

"I don't like you s-spittin' in a bottle after 3 O'clock." she said weakly. "From now on you can spit all you want."

"O.K. Captain Hunter. That's good enough for me. Turn to a heading of two seven zero and follow me."

Chapter Thirty-Five
Aftermath

September 11, 2001 / 09:47 EST / Cleveland Hopkins International Airport.

"The world will never be the same."

- Anonymous

Her hands stung. They were rubbed raw from sliding down the nylon emergency escape strap that dangled from the cockpit window. When she hit the ground a spike of pain shot through one misplaced ankle. Kelly was grateful for the distraction. It was an anchor point in the controlled chaos that surrounded her. Sirens screamed. Emergency vehicles with flashing lights and FBI and SWAT vehicles swarmed around her like angry hornets. Shouting people were everywhere. People from her plane were being shoved face down on the ground as if they had been the terrorists. Kelly didn't like it, but she could understand the necessity. For all the police knew, they were the terrorists.

Kelly had taxied the aircraft to a remote section of Cleveland's Airport where a bomb would do the least damage. Then she was ordered out of the cockpit via the captain's emergency exit side window. Heavily armed men in black body armor rushed her as soon her feet hit the tarmac.

"Down on the ground! Hands on head! Hands on head!" Insistent voices barked instructions. Kelly placed her hands on her head and slid to the ground compliantly. Big gloved hands that smelled of leather and gun oil pushed her face down into position on the tarmac. A knee was on her back, keeping her pinned. Other shouts echoed commands near her aircraft.

Until the officials could sort out the terrorists from the victims everyone was assumed to be a threat. Kelly knew they wanted pilots off the plane first to keep it grounded, but she hated leaving her crew and passengers. Irrationally, she felt like a coward. *Captains do not abandon their ships or their people!* she thought angrily.

The hot asphalt jammed pieces of tar and gravel into her cheek. Dust laced with oily fumes worked its way into her nose. She squeezed her eyes shut and let her body sink into the warm sticky surface. A tear of relief scalded an embarrassing path down her face. Kelley had already radioed in the number of passengers, crewmembers, and terrorists. She'd been very specific on the fact that Fletch was an Air Marshal. She hoped no mistakes would be made.

"Captain Kelly Hunter?" The question sounded more like a military roll call confirming her status. She turned her head slightly to see the legs of a black clad team leader standing over her. She followed them up to a well camouflaged visage. He looked back and forth between a slip of paper in his hand and her face. Two other Cleveland Police SWAT members kept their H&K MP 5 rifles trained on her.

"Yes sir." she responded. "I'm Captain Hunter."

"This dispatch says you have two of the hijackers subdued and restrained on board the aircraft. Is that correct?"

"Yes. We have them wrapped in duct tape and plastic cuffs." Kelly confirmed.

Incredulity crept between the lines of his next clipped question. "Then this is not a hostage situation?"

"No. This is no longer a hostage situation." Kelley said. "There is a Federal Air Marshal on board. Two hijackers and my first officer are dead. Several of my flight attendants and a passenger are dead or injured. One terrorist is wearing a Delta pilot uniform. He killed my first officer. He tried to kill me and take over the aircraft. If you want to get any information out of him, I suggest you get him to a hospital ASAP." *I hope he dies slowly and painfully.* Kelly thought. She couldn't help thinking it. A primal vengeful, angry, and grief-stricken part of her wished it.

"The other one is still unconscious." she repeated wearily. "We secured them both with zip ties and duct tape and dragged them into the forward galley. The last time I looked, we were still in control of the aircraft." Puffs of dust punctuated her words as she spoke. Her face was still wedged against the ground.

The dark figure looming over her considered this as he confirmed her identity with the photo in his hand. "Sorry captain." he apologized. "We weren't informed of this." He motioned to the other two men who lowered their weapons and helped her up. She stood on rubbery legs as the men steadied her.

Muttering something about bureaucratic miscommunications, the team leader brought the radio to his mouth and informed his people of a change in plans. Kelley couldn't tell if this was meant as an explanation to her or his way of cursing all the other agencies that were scurrying around vying for control of the situation.

"Are you in need of medical attention ma'am, er -captain?" the SWAT leader asked.

"Not immediately. Most of this blood isn't mine. I can wait. Please." she said. "Go see to my people." As if responding to her request, groups of armed SWAT teams had positioned themselves in strategic areas around the aircraft. Others rushed up the air stairs as the forward entry door popped open. Kelley could hear shouts of "Hands on heads! Remain seated!" as they disappeared into the interior. Moments later, medical personnel followed with stretchers and first aid kits.

Kelley started to walk toward the plane, concerned about her crew, her passengers and Fletch. She'd had to leave so rapidly she had no idea what their status was since they landed.

"I'm sorry captain. You can't do that." The SWAT leader gripped her arm gently but firmly. "You will all be debriefed separately. No contact right now." Kelley understood, but she didn't like it. Running on adrenalin, shock, frayed nerves, and mixed emotions she knew she probably wasn't thinking straight and should just do as the man said.

"I don't understand why I couldn't stay with my aircraft when the situation was under control" she said. The team leader pulled his mask away revealing deceptively good-natured features.

"We didn't know that at the time. Even if we did, we still have to follow protocol out of an abundance of caution." he explained, tightening his grip. "Standard operating procedures for us. We have no say in the matter." Kelly looked like she was considering heading back to the aircraft again. "You'll be staying here with two of my men for now." He turned and jogged to the 767, leaving Kelley standing in anxious resignation between her bodyguards.

"The Federal Air Marshal is Eugene Fletcher!" she shouted after him. "He's one of the good guys. Don't shoot him!" Kelley was feeling paranoid at this point.

Fletch sat with his hands on his head and fingers comfortably laced together. Everyone still able to move was doing the same thing. He knew what to expect and had explained the situation to the passengers and crew over the P.A. Emotional shock waves shuddered through the survivors when Shaheera opened the door and SWAT teams poured through.

A Kevlar clad torso stationed itself next to Fletch. The voice repeating the "hands on head" mantra. Fletcher grinned up into the stern features. The eyes moved to the FAM identification Fletch had clipped to his pocket, then back to his face. "Federal Air Marshal Eugene Fletcher?" the man demanded.

"Yes sir." Fletch responded. "Welcome aboard."

The SWAT leader looked back into the galley at Hamid Bin Laden's ghoulishly ravaged features. He gestured toward the wheezing terrorist with his chin. "You do that?"

"No. The captain did that. I think we'd better get a medical team up here fast if you want to interrogate him." Fletch suggested.

The officer lowered his gaze to the man on the floor and grimaced at the smell of urine that surrounded Jamal. "What happened to this one?" the officer asked, looking at Jamal's sorry condition. "I've only seen extreme pain, fear or both make a man lose bladder control. Did the captain do that too?"

"No. I did that." Fletch swiveled his head to look at the team leader. The movement had a wolfish look to it. "He got up again and we had a political discussion."

The LEO gave him a slight nod of approval and moved on. "You look like you could use some medical attention yourself." he stated. "You can lower your hands now. Do you realize you've been cut?" Fletch looked down at his shredded shirt. The bleeding wound across his rib cage began to hurt as soon as he acknowledged it and his adrenalin rush subsided. He felt light headed and lowered his hands to tuck a blanket firmly between his chest and arm.

The SWAT leader looked back at Hamid. "Your guy's lucky it was you that had the talk with him instead of the captain. What did you do? Threaten to turn her loose on him?" A shadow crossed his face. "You're the only plane that didn't crash today." The officer's eyes carried a haunted look behind them.

Fletcher's relaxed composure stiffened. He felt like ice water was flooding his veins. "What do you mean the only plane? Was there another one?"

The SWAT leader hesitated as if reviewing operational protocol. "No one's told you what's happening?" He lowered his voice and proceeded to fill a stunned Fletch in on the unreal events of the morning. "So far two commercial airliners have hit the World Trade Center. Another one just hit the Pentagon. As of a few minutes ago, United flight 93 might have crashed in Pennsylvania. We don't know how many more are being hijacked. The whole Aviation system of the United States is shutting down." The man suddenly looked older. "You're the last one we know of and the only one with survivors and a couple of live Tangos. The Feds will be overjoyed."

Fletch closed his eyes and swallowed past the lump in his throat. He'd done what he could. The scope of the attack was beyond anything he'd imagined. "Does Kelly, Captain Hunter know?"

The SWAT leader shook his head. "I probably shouldn't even be talking to you. Consider it a professional courtesy." he said by way of explanation. "Just between you and me." The intensity of their conversation had momentarily tuned the others out.

"Coming through!" a harried paramedic pushed up the aisle past them. The SWAT officer moved out of the way and turned back to supervising his team.

Fletch continued sitting in stunned silence. Thinking about what he'd forced the terrorist Jamal to reveal. *I probably know more about what happened today than anyone, Al Qaeda included.* he realized. Fletch felt incredibly alone. His arms ached to hold his children, and Kelley.

An ocean of activity surged around him as paramedics came on board examining the wounded and triaging them in the order of who should be taken off first. Hoarse wheezes emanated from Hamid Bin Laden's position. He was blocked from view by technicians performing an emergency tracheotomy. Select pieces of medical gear shuffled back and forth to the rhythm of clinical requests. Fletch hoped Hamid lived. He'd be an invaluable source of information to fight or prevent the future attacks Fletch knew would come. Medical personnel started toward the rear of the aircraft with Jamal's litter.

"You can't come out this way." a SWAT member advised them. "The bomb squad's working here." Fletch had tied the dead bomber's wrists to one of the aisle seats in an area where the least damage would be done to the aircraft. The detonating device was secured with duct tape, pillows, blankets and belts. Coach passengers had already been moved away from him and would be exiting from the aft doors.

The paramedics hefted Hamid out on a stretcher and struggled down the stairs from the forward entry door. Local and Federal law enforcement waited at the bottom of the stairs. Each insisted on their right to secure the areas with crime scene tape.

"Time to go Agent Fletcher." His SWAT escort had returned. "You and the captain will be the first in for debriefing. Someone claiming to be Bob is insisting on sitting in on the process as well." Fletch rose and stood painfully.

"If you're asking, Bob's' fine with me." Fletch said. "Bob is Lt. Colonel Robert. S. Blakely II, FAM Liaison to the White House and a welcome addition to sit in on the debriefing."

The team leader shrugged. "It's not up to me. I just thought you'd like to know." Fletch nodded his thanks and moved up the aisle. Passing the dignified older couple, he caught the eye of the silver haired gentleman. The man smiled at him with a strange mix of gratitude and serene certainty. Fletch got the impression the man knew something he didn't.

"No talking." the SWAT officer reminded them. "Keep moving." Fletch looked away and allowed himself to be herded down the stairs and into an armored vehicle. His Kevlar clad escort closed the doors and buckled in beside him.

"Any idea who that gentleman was?" Fletch asked.

The SWAT officer looked at the ceiling and sighed. "I guess I might as well be hung for a sheep as a goat." he said. "That's

Spencer Sterling and his wife, Sylvia Sterling. Arguably one of the three wealthiest couples in the world. You wouldn't know it by his lifestyle. They're very private and very influential people on the world chess board. Smart. Innovative. I really don't know any more about them than that. He seemed to take an interest in you." Settling into his seat as the vehicle lurched into motion he added, "If you had to save someone's life that was certainly a good pick." That answer just added more questions to Fletcher's list. He turned to look out the window. The silver haired couple were being led down the stairs by an escort that looked more like Secret Service than SWAT.

Swiveling to the right, he saw Kelly being helped into a police vehicle as they passed. She was limping, but turned in time to see him. Kelly smiled at him. He knew he wasn't alone. Fletch settled into his seat and began to organize his thoughts for the grueling debriefing ahead of him. The FBI would be doing the interrogation. That was the proper word for it. There was an adversarial relationship between that agency and other branches of law enforcement, FAM's included. The information he'd obtained involving national security would be taken and used, but his methods of obtaining it could be used against him. He hoped Shaheera and the Sterlings wouldn't mention it.

They drove away from the 767 toward a hanger that had been cordoned off for the debriefing of passengers and crew. A small government business jet was parked next to it. Fletch relaxed at the sight of the familiar bulldog-like silhouette of a man standing by the door. Bob had found a way to be in the right place at the right time, for Fletcher's sake.

"Mind if I touch base with my FAM Liaison first?" Fletch asked, reaching for the door handle. He had no doubt the request would be granted. There was a mutual support system between front line Law Enforcement Officers when the FBI was involved.

"Make it quick." the SWAT officer replied as he tapped the driver and motioned a stop. Bob started toward the vehicle then turned and walked back to the airplane, waiting for Fletch to come to him. Fletch took the hint and went to his friend.

"How did you get here so fast?" Fletch asked, slowing to a walk. "I thought the airspace was shut down."

Bob looked pale, and relieved to see him. "I had second thoughts about sending you off on that flight without your firearm." he said. "I was already enroute to meet you and detain Atta in Los Angeles when the planes started going down." Bob brought his hand up to his face as if to wipe away the awful reality. "We were tracking your flight anyway, so we landed here. God. I'm sorry Fletch." He looked up with regret. "I believed you, but I didn't have authority to do more. Becoming a bureaucrat makes cowards of us all." he said with self-loathing.

Fletch stopped and leaned against the airplane. "You're scaring me Bob." he said in mock horror. "I'm going to need the good old pit bull FAM advocate to deal with the FBI, not a puppy dog. Don't go all sentimental on me. You did the right thing or we'd have had five smoking holes in the ground instead of four." Fletch grinned and readjusted his bloody blanket. Bob shuffled uncomfortably.

"Let's do it then." he said. Bob straightened up to his familiar military posture. "Tell me what happened and I'll run interference." Bob gave Fletch a long-suffering look.

"Your methods are effective, but unorthodox to say the least." He looked at the SWAT leader in the car and suggested "We'd better keep it short. Your escort's getting nervous."

Fletch nodded at the team leader and indicated that he'd be right back. "What happened to Flight 11?" he asked, remembering turning back to Kelly's flight as Atta boarded the American jet.

"It hit the North Tower of the World Trade Center." Bob answered. Fletch was suddenly blind-sided with guilt. He couldn't have been in both places at once.

Bob saw the expression and asked "Atta?"

"He boarded Flight 11 instead of Delta Flight 1989." Fletch answered succinctly. Bob grunted understanding.

"Water under the bridge." he advised. "You picked the better option. You know I have to ask you this before someone else does. Did you use any unorthodox methods of obtaining information from the Tangos while subduing them?"

Fletch didn't hesitate. "I used the necessary force subdue and restrain them. One was very vocal in the process."

"That's our answer and we're sticking to it." Bob nodded in assent. "Witnesses?" he asked.

"Just the elderly couple up front and the lead flight attendant, Shaheera. I think she's also Kelly Hunters best friend. I don't think she has any grudges against me. At least I hope not." Fletch replied. "I have a good feeling about the Sterlings. That pair have more street smarts than you'd expect, and they appear to be grateful."

"Very well then." Bob replied, looking at the bloody blanket. "Get that taken care of and I'll see you inside."

"It's good to have you here." Fletch said by way of thanks.

Bob grinned. "You're welcome." Both men turned to go into the hanger. Fletch was trailed by the armored SWAT vehicle and an ambulance.

Kelly's FBI transport pulled up just as Fletch entered the building, but not before he had a chance to look at her, smile and put his hand over his heart. She thought he couldn't have been more eloquent. She'd need that reassurance later. The world had changed and no one had told her yet.

"Come with me Captain Hunter." her escort said, opening her door. She rose gingerly on her damaged ankle and followed him into the hanger.

Chapter Thirty-Six
Vanishing Act

September 11, 2001 – 11:45am

"This is a nasty, rotten business."

**- Robert L. Crandall, President and
CEO, American Airlines**

The holding area echoed with disturbing rumors. People huddled in tense groups, besieged by the non-stop screams of jets and smaller aircraft landing as the sky emptied. Cleveland International Airport was overwhelmed with airliners diverting to the nearest suitable airports. An undercurrent of fear and tension filled the building.

"Please." Kelly begged. "I've been here for three hours. Bad things are happening out there. I need to call my son." The paramedic splinting her ankle looked inquiringly at the FBI agent she was talking to. Kelly attempted to reach the human being behind the sunglasses. "I need to know that my son's all right." she repeated. The man stared back, Hands clasped in front of his neat white

Arrow shirt. It was maddening. She thought he wasn't' going to answer. He removed the Ray Bans and placed them carefully in his pocket. His eyes were an impenetrable hazel.

"That isn't possible." he stated. The remark was pure business. A slight tightening of the skin around his mouth was the only sign that he knew Kelly was fighting back panic. The paramedic shook his head and went back to applying an ice pack to her swelling ankle.

"She just wants to call her kid." the paramedic muttered under his breath. "Have a heart." The agent's answering glare was enough to silence him. "Sorry." the paramedic said, returning his attention to her injury. "It's none of my business".

The hazel eyes turned back to Kelly.

"I have kids of my own." He turned the same unflappable look on her but his voice had softened. "I can only tell you that your son knows you're O.K. It's been on the news. We've contacted him. He's fine and staying with relatives."

"Thank you." Kelly winced as the bandage was tightened. "The FBI interviewed me for an hour and I've been sitting here for another two. This has been ... a hard day. When can I go home?" she asked. The man plucked the sunglasses from his pocket and put them back on.

"Not until the FBI releases you, Captain Hunter." the agent replied. "That won't happen until everyone's been interviewed and we decide what to do with you."

"What do you mean 'until you decide what to do with me'"? Kelly asked.

The FBI agent had resumed his "I'm a robot" stance and refused to look at her. "I'm not at liberty to discuss that ma'am." She almost laughed at the cliché. It was obvious that this was the end of the discussion.

Kelly clenched her teeth in frustration. She wondered if the FBI was thinking of pressing assault charges against her on Hamid's behalf. The interview had been strange. Almost as if they were trying to figure out if she'd committed some crime. Kelly was still trying to assimilate the events of the day. The more she knew, the less real it all seemed. Her mind finally settled on being comfortably numb. She looked at the door Fletch had gone through two hours ago and wondered what was taking so long. He was in no shape to be raked over the coals. "I thought we were the good guys." she muttered under her breath.

The door swung open. A heavy-set man with a clipboard, wing tip shoes and reading glasses ushered an exhausted Fletch out. His chest was bandaged and blood had seeped through the dressing in crimson rosettes.

"Get that taken care of Marshal. We'll want to talk more about this later." the interrogator advised him. He turned and motioned for the next flight crew member to follow him into the room. Fletch saw Kelly and stumbled as he started toward her. His blood loss was finally taking its toll.

"Where do you think you're going Captain?" the paramedic asked as Kelly tried to stand. Her ankle was doing its best imitation of a grapefruit and it refused to support her. She wobbled on one foot as a muscular man with an attitude appeared to help support Fletch. Bob hadn't been permitted to sit in on the interrogation, and he wasn't happy about it.

"You. - Sit," the technician ordered Kelly. She sat obediently. "And you." he ordered Bob. "Bring the Air Marshal over here and put him on this cot. He needs medical attention." Bob did as he was told and helped Fletch lay down next to Kelly's chair. "Any objections?" the paramedic asked their FBI watchdog. The agent shrugged a "no."

Having assumed control of the situation, the medical technician turned to Fletch, checked his bandages and prepared an IV drip. Bob paced around them like a nervous father.

"Hi." Kelly said, taking Fletcher's free hand in both of hers. Smiling into his eyes she held his hand to her heart. His skin was cold. She warmed it against hers and relief flooded her body. Fletch gripped her hand tighter and smiled back, seeing nothing but Kelly.

"Hi."

She reached out and smoothed the bloody matted hair back from his face. Her fingers caressed his jaw line. She leaned forward and placed her mouth gently on his. Fletch pulled her closer, wanting it to never end.

"Damn. I knew I should have gone into the Air Marshal Service." the FBI Agent blurted out. He'd taken his Ray Bans off and was staring at Kelly and Fletch. Surprised at his own outburst he looked around, hoping no one heard him. Then the sunglasses went back on. Kelly sat up and scowled at him, still holding Fletcher's hand. Fletch would have blushed if he had any blood to spare for the process. All eyes turned to the FBI agent who was trying to blend into the wall.

"Ha, - Ow!" An aborted laugh caught Fletch as he tried to lift himself up on one elbow and breathe. "Hurts when I laugh." he observed.

"Where does it hurt?" the paramedic asked.

"Ribs specifically. Everywhere in general." Fletch replied. "Except here." he added, grinning and pointing to his mouth.

"Could be a broken or bruised rib." the medic advised. "No more laughing." He smiled as he said it, enjoying the brief respite from tragedy. Bob stopped his pacing and was studying Kelly. He dragged a folding chair to the other side of the cot and sat down.

"I'm Lt. Colonel Robert Blakely." He said, extending his hand to Kelly. "It's a pleasure to meet you, Captain Hunter." Kelly looked at him with curiosity. Bob realized she had no clue who he was. "My apologies." he offered. "You probably think I'm FBI. I'm not. I'm the FAM Liaison to the White House Situation Room. A friend of Fletchers, and the idiot who almost fired him for insisting on protecting you."

Kelly sized up the big man sitting across from her with mixed emotions. "You almost fired Fletch for protecting me?" she repeated. Her eyes narrowed. Bob looked like he could eat nails for breakfast but the sight of him waiting for her approval with eyes that begged forgiveness finally won her over. She smiled and took his proffered hand. "It's good to meet you too Colonel Blakely. Did anyone ever tell you that those puppy dog eyes work well on women?"

Bob took her hand and patted it. "My wife does all the time." he chuckled. "I'm just glad it worked on you too."

"Hey! Get your own Airline Captain." Fletch interjected. "This one's taken."

"Stop using the term "puppy dog" when referring to me and I might consider backing off." Bob growled.

"Don't make him laugh." the medic warned, lining up a vein on Fletcher's arm to insert the I.V. needle.

The door to the interrogation room opened again, expelling another shell-shocked crew member. The heavy-set man motioned a bandaged Shaheera in. She was trailed by a smitten EMT who was turned away at the door. Shaheera gave a small wave to Kelly and disappeared inside the room as the FBI interrogator said something reassuring to her and closed the door. Kelly waved back and wondered if the man had any idea who he was dealing with.

She let go of Fletcher's hand so he could drink some orange juice, and tilted her head to listen. A sudden eerie quiet had settled over them. All aircraft had landed, somewhere. The sky was vacant. No one was going anywhere for a long time. The silence intensified the sounds in the hanger. They were being held in a sterile environment with no news other than what the SWAT leader and the FBI agent had told them. It was nerve wracking.

"Agent Hagar." a man across the room raised his voice and directed it at their FBI watchdog. "I need to speak with you." The agent headed for his supervisor and began an animated discussion before he was handed a phone. He put it to his ear and cast several curious looks back in their direction. Then he devoted his full attention to what was being said on the other end.

Bob took advantage of the man's absence. "Something strange is going on here." he told them. "I watched CNN and other news stations in the jet while you were being interrogated." he said. "All of them are reporting that your flight #1989 was not hijacked." Kelly looked puzzled and scooted her chair closer, glancing at the preoccupied FBI agent. Fletch put his orange juice down and turned an interested face to Bob who clasped his hands on his knees and continued. "They're saying the hijacking of Delta flight 1989 was a false alarm caused by an unruly passenger who refused to turn off his cell phone."

"The T.V. station must have made a mistake." Kelly said "It's been a confusing day everywhere."

"They're all reporting the same thing." Fletch observed. "It's not a mistake."

"That's the information the authorities are giving them?" Kelly asked incredulously.

"I knew you were smart." Bob said. "That's the information the media is being fed. It's going to be interesting to see how the people behind this cover-up intend to deal with the passengers and crew who were involved in the real thing."

"You mean when they decide what to do with us?" Kelly stated ominously. "This is getting scary. What's going on?"

Kelly and Fletcher both looked to Bob for an answer.

"I wish I knew. Unfortunately, my job description doesn't take me into those rarified realms of National Security." Bob looked past Fletch to the FBI agent who was walking back to them. "Maybe we're about to find out."

The sunglasses were off. *That's a good sign.* Kelly thought. *When he has his Ray Bans on, he's Robo-Cop. Ray Bans off. Human being.* She thought the agent looked as puzzled as she felt. He stopped short of them and seemed to be gathering his thoughts. He looked at Fletch.

"Can this man be moved?"

"I don't know." Bob said. "Our medic is over there having coffee and a doughnut. Why?"

"Because you're no longer under the jurisdiction of the FBI. We need to transfer you to another location." Kelly looked alarmed and Fletch put his hand possessively on her thigh.

"Wherever she goes, I go." he stated.

"That makes three of us." Bob added. His aggressive posture brooked no argument. "Hold on people." the agent said, raising his hands a placating gesture. "You're all going together. A unit of the National Security Agency wants to talk to you. All I can do is get you there."

"Where exactly is 'there'?" Kelly asked suspiciously.

"They have a facility set up in another building at this airport." the agent replied. "They're sending a driver."

"If they're going to torture us, can I at least have a hot bath, a bed and a phone first?" Kelly asked facetiously. The agent looked at her with a blank stare.

"The NSA isn't allowed to torture you ma'am."

Fletch pulled her down and whispered. "Kelly, the FBI isn't issued a sense of humor."

Chapter Thirty-Seven
Psychological Warfare

*September 11, 2001 / late afternoon / Hopkins
Cleveland International Airport.*

"You don't know what you don't know."

-      **Flight Instructors favorite saying**

The office suite was enormous. It overlooked the East side of Cleveland and the crowded ramps of the airport. The luxurious surroundings made it a safe-haven from the chaos outside.

"This must be an executive board room for an airline." Bob commented from his recliner. "I wonder where our host is?" He took a sip of his coffee.

"Wherever he is, I'm glad he's taking his time. A little hot water and soap is pure heaven." Kelly was using the edge of a towel to clean Fletchers face and hands. He was comfortably propped up on a long leather couch, enjoying her attention.

"As much as I like this, you need to rest too Kelly." Fletch said. She was sitting in a chair next to him, with her foot up and packed in ice. Fletch slipped an arm around her waist and she nuzzled his clean cheek before lying back in her recliner. The soiled towel went into the bucket of warm water beside her.

A slim woman of indeterminate age stood by the door. She was dressed in a neat Polo pant suit and had arranged her dark hair in a French twist. "Can I get you anything else right now?" she asked solicitously. "Mr. Grey will be with you shortly."

"We'd appreciate any food you could come up with." Bob said. "I don't think these two have eaten anything all day. I know I haven't, and it's nearly six pm."

"I am so sorry." she apologized. "I assumed they had fed you. Will some sandwiches do?" she asked. "Food is in short supply with all of the people stranded here at the airport."

"Sandwiches will be just fine." Bob replied to her retreating figure. She opened the large mahogany doors and left as three men came in. Two of them were flanking a tall tanned gentleman in a grey flannel suit. He wore a wine-colored tie and sported a sharp white crew cut. The effect was a worldly masculine elegance. His dark suited companions looked familiar to Fletch. He recognized them as the same men who had escorted Mr. and Mrs. Sterling off the airplane.

"Thank you, gentlemen." the man said, dismissing the bodyguards. They turned and left, closing the doors quietly behind them.

"My name is Grey." he said, seating himself behind a deep red mahogany desk. "Would you prefer to wait until you've eaten something or would you like to know what all of this is about right now?" He smiled a brilliant white smile and waited for their answer. Kelly, Fletch and Bob gawked in unison.

"You don't beat around the bush, do you Mr. Grey?" Bob ventured "I think it's safe to say we'd all like to know what's going on." The other two nodded their heads in agreement.

"Good." Mr. Grey said. "First you need to embrace concept that this event never happened."

"What's that supposed to mean?" Bob asked. Grey leaned back in his chair and steepled his fingers. "As you said, I don't beat around the Bush. It's a waste of time and energy." he replied. "It is what it sounds like Lt. Colonel Blakely."

"But why?" Kelly asked. "How are we even supposed to do that? People were killed and wounded on my flight."

"Who are you anyway?" Fletch asked suspiciously. "Just what branch of the NSA do you work for?"

The brilliant smile flashed at them again. Then it vanished. Grey leaned forward, placing his elbows on the desk. "Those are good questions and I'll answer them all in that order." He poured himself a glass of the ice water provided on a tray next to him. "Make yourselves comfortable." he suggested as he touched some buttons on his desk. Blinds running the length of the picture windows slid shut, darkening the room. A large wall screen illuminated in front of them and the lights automatically dimmed. Kelly stared at it as an unwelcome face reconstructed itself. The face looked back with a self-satisfied smirk. Mr. Grey was watching her intently. "Do you recognize this man?"

"I killed him, didn't I?" Kelly said numbly. "Did he die?" The reality of what had happened was beginning to set in. Grey chuckled.

"No Captain Hunter. You didn't kill him. I have no doubt you could have, and it was close." Grey turned back to the screen. "The irony here is that you probably saved his miserable life. You're watching his suicide tape. This man is Hamid Bin Laden. One of Osama bin Laden's brothers." Grey focused a laser-like gaze on Kelly, who looked confused. "You delivered an invaluable source of information and leverage to us Captain Hunter. Are you familiar with who Osama bin Laden is?" Kelly nodded. "Vaguely familiar."

"I remember now. We were given his name in Security training and told that he was a terrorist with an interest in airlines." she said. "That's all. I thought the Bin Laden name sounded familiar when he came into the cockpit but I couldn't recall where I'd heard it. They kind of glossed over it." she added apologetically. Grey's expression turned grim. He spoke softly, almost to himself.

"That's changed. The whole world has changed today, and there will be very few people in it that won't know who Osama bin Laden is." He let the video continue in the background as he spoke. "A group headed by Bin Laden attacked the United States today. On our own soil. I assume you haven't had much information on this yet?" he added. They shook their heads "no".

"We only know that two commercial planes hit the World Trade Center and one hit the Pentagon." Fletch offered. "Fill us in." Kelly covered his hand with hers, comforted by the touch.

"The World Trade Towers are gone. Collapsed and vaporized in the collapse." he said. "Along with thousands of innocent civilians and the rescue teams trying to save them. The terrorists timed it that way deliberately." Grey closed his eyes and massaged his temples. Warding off a stress headache. "Hundreds more died in the Pentagon. United flight 93 crashed in a field in Pennsylvania. Apparently, the passengers intervened and the terrorists crashed the plane rather than letting the passengers in. We think it was intended for Capitol Hill and Congress."

Grey took a sip of ice water and continued, fixing them with a steely gaze. "Your flight with Osama's brother Hamid at the controls was intended to make an ideological statement. They wanted it to be the final insult that would drive the United States into attacking an Islamic country. That would polarize the Muslim populations of the world into Al Qaeda's radical belief system and against everyone else." He let what he'd said sink in." Your flight was supposed to hit the White House and paralyze the American people with fear while showing the rest of the world how vulnerable we are."

"Jesus." Fletch said softly.

"The gauntlet has been thrown down and this nation is engaged in a war like nothing we've ever faced before." Grey stated.

"Civilians are the targets. These people have no sense of honor or fair play. They don't abide by the Geneva Convention. Their objective is to control the world under a harsh Islamic rule by using terror. They employ lies and subterfuge to kill anyone who doesn't agree with their radical views. Nothing is sacred. It's going to get worse before it gets better."

This is a nightmare. Kelly thought. *Please, not in our children's time. Not ever.* Fletch felt her hands shaking and squeezed them reassuringly. His throat was dry. His thoughts turned to his own children.

"Here's the good news." Grey continued. "You not only survived and saved countless lives in the process, but you've just handed us a trump card in this nasty business. Osama bin Laden is probably watching the news right now and wondering what went wrong." Grey leaned forward and his grin went feral. "He wonders why he hasn't heard from his brother or about your flight hitting the White House. He's feeling vulnerable because he doesn't know what we know and what we don't about his operation. We need to keep it that way."

Bob let out a long low whistle. "The psychological warfare is that important?" he asked.

"Think about it. The monster in the dark is infinitely more frightening than the one you can see." Grey said. " Yes, it is that important. Future plans and safe havens that Bin Laden has are now in doubt. He was counting on his brother dying in the crash, so he probably shared information with Hamid that he wouldn't have shared otherwise."

"Do we have a choice in the matter?" Bob asked.

"Not really." Grey said. "We've already broadcast an official news account of a false hijack attempt on Delta Flight #1989. You had an unruly passenger with a cell phone he refused to turn off. It was just a misunderstanding. That's all." Grey's voice was still calm and companionable. "Your employers have agreed to go along with this story. It's in their own best interests to do so." he looked at them significantly. "Can you give me a reason why you would want to compromise this operation?"

"I don't like to lie." Kelly said. "Especially to my friends, family and my son." She hesitated, feeling trapped, and more than a little angry. "If I don't, it could put them in harm's way." She looked up at Grey. "Am I right?"

"Exactly." Grey agreed. "I think this story will be far less traumatic and troubling to them as well. "On the other hand, if you decided to contradict the accepted story you'll be viewed as a nut case and a liar. You would lose your job. People from a security agency would pay you a visit and clarify the consequences of violating national security." Grey smiled again. "I was hoping to elicit your co-operation on a voluntary basis.

"I was just asking." Bob replied.

"It makes sense to me." Fletch agreed. "But that's my job. I'm used to it." He looked at Kelly. "Is this what you want to do?" She nodded.

"Sounds like it's the only choice we have." They both looked at Bob. He nodded assent as well.

"What about the passengers and crew?" he asked. "How do you control that?"

"My first officer and two flight attendants are dead." Kelly said bitterly. "You can't explain that away."

"I've been in this business a long time." Grey commented. "It's easier than we like to think." He turned to Kelly with unexpected compassion. "Your co-pilot, one passenger in coach and your flight attendants died with honor, defending the flight. It's a shame they'll only be given credit for that in a small circle." he said. Kelly felt her eyes burning. She blinked back tears. Grey rolled the glass with the melted ice in his hands.

"Their names have been put on the passenger lists of the planes that went into the Towers, a field in Pennsylvania and the Pentagon. Your first officer was dead-heading on American flight 11 to pick up a flight in Los Angeles. For all anyone else knows, their bodies were incinerated." He looked at them with troubled eyes. "As I said. It's a dirty business. We have to play it by the rules the enemy sets." Grey took another swallow of water as if to rinse a bad taste from his mouth. "The rest of the passengers were from military families and government employees, or on the staff of Mr. Sterling and his wife. They understand the necessity for this ruse." His attention refocused on Kelly.

"Your crew members will be given this same speech. It's probably better if you don't speak about this with them, other than to confirm the story you are being given. Do you understand?"

Kelly nodded again. "Yes sir, I do." she felt bone crushingly weary as she asked "When can I go home?"

"Flight crews and passengers are stranded in hotels all over the United States. They will be for another few days. We'd like you to stay here for that time and under those pretenses for a thorough briefing on your stories. Then you can go home." He included Fletch in his statement. "You both need to get further medical treatment anyway, which we will provide." He looked at Kelly. "I'm told you have a spiral fracture on the tibia of your right ankle, Captain Hunter. You may need surgery. Maybe even a pin to stabilize it." He addressed his next comment to Fletch. "You may have a broken rib and you have a deep cut which also requires a surgeon's attention. This will work out just fine." he reassured them. "Looks like you'll both be out on job related sick leave for a month or so. That said, you're still going to be separated for a few days.

"What about me?" Bob asked.

"You know everything you need to know Lt. Colonel Blakely. You're needed back at the White House Situation room. They're aware of everything I've told you." Grey added." You don't have to stifle yourself."

"Do I look like I'm capable of stifling myself?" Bob said.

"Only when it's absolutely necessary." Grey granted. A light illuminated on his desk mounted panel and he pushed the intercom switch. "Yes?"

"I have your sandwiches and some fruit and chips sir. May bring them in?" "Give me a moment Susan. I'm sure they'll be I appreciated." Grey switched off the intercom and went back to business. "Robert. Stay and have a sandwich. Then I need to get you down to your jet ASAP. You have special clearance through the airspace to get you back to the White House." Bob looked at Kelly and Fletch, silently asking if they felt secure with his leaving now.

Fletch grinned. "Get back to work Bob. We'll be fine." He got the idea that Bob was going to make up for his guilt by being over-protective. "Bring in the food." Fletch added. "Unless you're trying to starve us into compliance."

The doors swung open for the woman bearing a heaping cart of sandwiches. The two men outside closed the doors behind her, making sure Grey and his audience weren't disturbed as they ate. Mr. Grey joined them with a ham and Swiss on rye. Then got up and encouraged Bob to be on his way. Hurried goodbyes and promises to keep in touch were exchanged before he was escorted out the door. Mr. Grey went through the motions of straightening his tie and running his fingers through hair cropped too close to matter.

"Your friend is a difficult man to maneuver." he commented. "I admire that. I needed a few minutes alone with you two," he explained, seating himself in Bob's vacated chair.

"Why is that?" Fletch asked. "You still haven't told us what branch of the NSA you work for." Kelly exchanged a melted bag of ice with a fresh one in the bucket and waited for his answer. Everything about this man pointed to power above levels she knew existed.

"We don't work for the NSA." he explained. "It would more accurate to say that we have a good working relationship with them. Right now, I'm representing them. You don't need to worry about dealing with anything outside of the scope of our government."

"Then who are you?" Fletch demanded.

"As I said, I represent the NSA. I'm also a close friend and employee of this man." He handed Fletch a card with a name and phone number on it. "He's independent, but has been an incalculable asset to this country." Grey handled the card as if it was a holy relic. "Mr. Sterling and his wife have taken quite a liking to you and Captain Hunter. They request the pleasure of your company at one of their retreats. This one is located in Taos, New Mexico."

"I think we both need to get home and check on our kids." Fletch stated, taking the card. I'm sure you understand. These are unsettling times." Kelly nodded in agreement. She was glad Fletch understood.

"Of course." Grey said sympathetically. "He wouldn't think of imposing on you until you've had a week or so to recover and see your families." He fixed them with a penetrating look that had good will behind it. Kelly noticed that his eyes were steel grey. She wondered if his name was a real one, or a pseudonym he'd picked because he liked the color.

"If I were you, I wouldn't pass up this opportunity." he said. "At the very least, you'll have a wonderful time and meet two of the world's finest people. If you stay the full week of your invitation, you'll be given a broader understanding of what just happened today and how we can deal with it effectively in the future." He handed another card to Kelly. "You understand this phone number and information is strictly confidential. Call when you decide on a convenient date and Mr. Sterling will arrange to have you picked up."

Fletch raised a questioning eyebrow to Kelly, thinking he really needed a peaceful week with her somewhere.

"I think we'd like that Mr. Grey." Kelly responded. "Especially since it doesn't look like we'll have much time together here." The twinkle returned to her eyes as she asked Fletch. "How long do you need to recover Fletcher?"

"I don't think I can stand waiting more than a week or two after they let us go to see you again Kelly. Neither one of us looks like we'll be going back to work any time soon." he said. "Can you swing the full week in Taos?"

She grinned in anticipation. "I think my son will be tired of me by then. I can stay the full week."

"May I tell the Sterlings to expect you?" Grey asked.

"Yes." Fletch replied, unable to tear his eyes away from Kelly. "Please thank them for us and tell them we're looking forward to it."

"You won't regret it." Grey said, helping himself to another sandwich. "It will change your lives".

Taos

September 25, 2001/ 09:30am MDT / Taos New Mexico / Restricted area / Sterling Ranch

"The same Chinese character is used to express both Crisis and Opportunity."

- Sun Tsu

Fletch drew the white cotton sheet closer to his nose. It held the cleansing scents of desert mornings. Sage, juniper, dew moistened earth, and Kelly. He breathed it in, filling his lungs with the healing fragrances.

The distant keening of a hawk rode a hint of wood smoke into the room. Kelly lay nestled against his chest. He smiled and pulled the comforter up over her bare shoulder. Pinion pine log beams graced the white-washed ceiling. One wall was an open floor to ceiling vista of the sprawling desert valley below. Fresh wildflowers and juniper branches sat in a simple vase on the mantle. Everything was casual Southwestern elegance. Including the Navaho blanket and comforter on the California king bed.

Fletch smiled and settled himself more comfortably under the covers. He and Kelly had been through Hell-on-earth. Both had been suffering sleepless nights, nightmares, hyper-vigilance, and other symptoms of Post Traumatic Stress since their brutal brush with death on 9/11. Depression, regret, and survivors guilt, feeling they should have done more and saved the people who'd died around them.

They, like everyone else in America and the world, had been bombarded 24/7 with horrific images of the deaths of over 3,000 people and the self-sacrifices of first responders, civilians like Todd Beamer, and the passengers and flight attendants on flight 93. Being together to comfort and talk it through was a balm to their tattered souls. They had slept peacefully for the first time in weeks.

Fletch thought this moment was Heaven-on-earth. They'd been gifted this beauty, peace, and healing together by the Sterlings.

Fletch and Kelly had seen the broad view of the Sterling's home two days ago, when their host's private helicopter approached the hidden helipad in the cliff wall. Their first impression was one of breathtaking grandeur. The residence was carved into the sheer face of a massive stone precipice. It formed itself around the natural setting like some contemporary version of an ancient Anasazi cliff dwelling. The place had a mystical feel about it. *There would be time to ask questions later.* Fletcher thought. He was content to relax and enjoy the serene ambiance of the moment.

A vast desert landscape peeked through the haze of Kelly's hair. He smiled and buried his nose in the fragrant spot behind her ear, letting the events of September 11th slip away. Fletch closed his eyes and listened to the silence. Moments later a clap of thunder boomed across the valley and echoed against the surrounding cliffs.

"Mmmm." Kelly purred. "Are we going to have another rainstorm?" The guest quarters were almost level with the clouds that chased each other over the desert below. A breath of wet sage and desert earth preceded the moisture.

"Yes. Rain." he said. "I certainly hope so." A smile teased at the corner of his mouth as he remembered last night's sudden downpour. It had driven them inside to a crackling pinion pine fire and the intimacy they'd both been starved for. Fletch ran a finger languorously down Kelly's cheek.

"Are you hungry?" he asked. "We forgot dinner last night." Kelly sat up and encouraged him to lean back, cradling him against her chest.

"You just want to play with the Sterling's high-tech gadget again." She chuckled and handed him the keypad. "Yes, I'm hungry. You always make me hungry." Kelly smiled. Fletch grinned and pulled her arms around him. Kelly's fingers traced the fresh scar healing on his chest. They both looked across the whitewashed room to the simple alcove by the table. Interesting things had been happening there. Meals would appear in the space at the touch of a key pad. Seemingly out of thin air. The remnants vanished just as quickly when they were done. It was intriguing to say the least.

"How does it do that?" Fletch wondered out loud. They'd brushed their hands across the surface searching for telltale cracks or obstructions and found none. The meals wouldn't appear until anything placed on the surface was removed. Their order would materialize almost instantaneously. Hot, fresh, and delicious.

"Matter transfer?" Fletch suggested half-heartedly, humming a few bars from "The Twilight Zone".

"I don't think so." Kelly said. "But I have no other explanation." *She wondered who their hosts really were and why she and Fletch were being shown these things.* "We'll ask the Sterlings about it tonight at dinner. It was nice of them to give us time to relax, but I'm ready to socialize and get some answers.

Fletcher nodded. "The Sterlings seem like great people, but they didn't invite us here and show us these things out of simple gratitude and courtesy. They have an agenda." Kelly added.

"Exactly." Fletch agreed. "I'm dying of curiosity, now that I've satisfied my craving for you."

Kelly laughed, flattered. "Oh you have, have you?"

"At least until after breakfast." Fletch replied. "What do you want to eat?"

"Strawberries, coffee, an avocado omelet and whole wheat toast, I'm starving." she said. Both of them had lost weight and their appetites since 9/11. They'd come back with a vengeance, along with their enthusiasm for life and each other. Fletch touched a preselected menu pad twice. "Juevos Rancheros again?" Kelly laughed.

"Good guess." Fletch replied. "Am I really that predictable?"

"Yup." Kelly and Fletch looked at each other and the clock.

"Sixty seconds." Kelly guessed.

"Ninety." Fletch countered.

"You're on." They settled back to watch the time and the vacant alcove. Kelly rested her chin on Fletcher's shoulder. Another unknown nagged at her mind. "Did you notice how quiet our helicopter got when we crossed into restricted airspace?" she asked.

"I noticed that." Fletch replied. "I'm not familiar enough with advanced rotorcraft to know if it was unusual or not."

"I flew them for the police years ago." Kelly said. "This one wasn't that different. The sudden seamless transition to quiet was unusual. Even the engine vibration stopped. If the rotors hadn't still been spinning, I would have thought we'd had engine failure."

"Maybe it's a new noise muffling system." Fletch suggested.

"I think it's more than that." Kelly ventured. "I know it sounds crazy, but I don't think the engine was running after we entered the Sterling Ranch restricted area."

"You're the expert." Fletch replied. "That's another question for tonight." He shook his head in bewilderment. "The things I've seen in this room alone are enough to convince me that anything's possible in this place." He continued staring at the alcove. His mind worried a mystery until he'd shaken it apart and reassembled the pieces into an understandable picture. Fletch couldn't help it. "Here's another anomaly for you." he said.

"The patio's wet with rain but our floor is dry as a bone and the room temperature is nice and cozy." *Their room had the option of glass pocket doors that slid out of sight into the wall on request, leaving the room open to the outside.* "The doors were open all night. What do you think that's about?" He squinted at the alcove, afraid to miss anything relevant. "Maybe I'm beginning to imagine things?" he added doubtfully.

"No. I think you're right." Kelly replied. "You're not imagining it. It's a very subtle sort of, magic, for lack of a better word." She said. "This place is elegantly simple. It fits here naturally. Yet it has this - technology?" she searched for the right word.

"Aww missed it again!" Fletch said. The food was there. They'd been watching as it appeared and there was nothing gradual about it. The effect was startling. "How long did that take?" he asked.

"About seventy seconds." Kelly estimated.

" "We both win." Fletcher grinned.

"We certainly do." Kelly said. "Pass the omelet and coffee please." She understood Fletcher's frustration. "The Sterling's wouldn't give us a show like this without intending to give us the answers later."

"I hope not." Fletch stated. "Because I can't leave here without knowing." He rolled slowly off the bed, favoring his bruised ribs and focused on the meal. "I'll get it." he suggested. "You should stay off that ankle." Fletch added "I've been wanting to serve you breakfast in bed for a long time."

He picked up her tray and walked back to the bed. More pinion pine logs materialized stacked on the patio. "This is nice." Fletch said. Noticing the logs at the same time Kelly did. "But it's getting a little unnerving." Kelly nodded in agreement. They both wondered why they'd trusted the Sterlings enough to allow themselves to be isolated here. Their PTSD made it harder to trust anyone but each other. Fletch put her serving tray on the bed and went back for his.

"Thank you." Kelly said, as she reached for the coffee. "Interesting. With all this technology available, we're still left to do simple tasks for ourselves. I think it's deliberately designed that way."

Fletch gave her an inquisitive look. "How so?" he asked.

"This technology is amazing, but not crippling or addictive. It encourages free choice and the enjoyment of interacting with each other and our surroundings. The ability to be alive in the moment." She took a bite of her perfectly ripened strawberry, savoring it. You know," she said. "The things that really make our lives rich and fulfilling. Our need for real social interaction with each other, our purpose. This technology preserves our humanity."

Fletch considered the idea for a moment. He slid his own tray onto the bed and climbed under the covers with her. "Now that's a novel thought." he said. "Power and humanity. I think we should move our meeting with the Sterlings forward to lunch." he proposed. "It all seems benign enough but I don't think I can wait until dinner for answers."

"A man after my own heart." she observed. "I like immediate gratification too."

"Hurry up and eat." Fletch suggested "I want to try out that natural hot spring on the terrace."

"Kelly grinned and bit into another strawberry. "I'm hurrying!"

* * *

Silvia Sterling was a beautiful woman. Even at the age of sixty-five. She moved down the stairs with grace and a warm smile. Her long silver hair complemented the silver Navajo Concho belt that cinched her waist. A simple white blouse, ankle length blue velvet skirt and the tiny set of beaded moccasins that peeked out from under it completed the charming effect that was Sylvia. She put a platter of enchiladas on the sandstone table next to the fresh salad and corn bread.

"Prepared from scratch." she told them. "I raise the tomatoes and herbs myself." she added. "They just don't have the same vine ripened flavor from the store."

"I am an indulged man." Spencer Sterling said. His wife bent down and planted a kiss on his cheek. He patted the hand she placed on his shoulder. "Silvia equates fresh cooking with love." He looked up at her fondly. "It's a good thing she plans a healthy menu, or I'd weigh three hundred pounds."

Kelly thought that was hardly the case. The gentleman sitting across from her resembled a healthy version of what the Marlborough Man might have looked like after six decades. Two streaks of white hair at his temples were the only concessions to age in his otherwise full head of well-groomed black hair. His denim jeans and cowboy boots appeared to be a functional set of clothes, rather than an affectation. *These two look like they were born for each other.* she thought. Her heart was glad for them. Kelly enjoyed seeing long-married couples who were so obviously still in love. Fletch reached under the table and twined his fingers with hers. Warmth flowed through her. She was deeply and completely loved too.

"Kelly and I want to thank you for your hospitality." Fletch said. "Your home is incredible. He looked at Kelly and shared a smile. We both needed the time away together." He hadn't figured out how to couch his questions without blurting them out and seeming rude.

Sterling nodded and stood to seat his wife. "We're delighted you two accepted our invitation. We owe you both a great deal." he gave them a lopsided grin. "But that's not the only reason we invited you." he continued. "We like exceptional people." Both Kelly and Fletch looked pleased, but at a loss for an appropriate response.

"Thank you for the compliment." Kelly replied.

"You are most welcome and deserving of it." Sylvia said. "It's both a compliment and an observation of fact." Silvia continued filling their plates with salad.

"Believe it." Sterling said. "Silvia is a Menschenkennerin."

Seeing their perplexed looks, Sylvia explained the concept as she sliced the hot corn bread. "That's just a German word for someone who has a knack for figuring people out, or taking their measure. Roughly translated it means: *A knower of people.* There are a few of us around." Sylvia licked a dollop of honey off her finger. "I worked for the CIA psy-ops division under Director Angleton during the cold war." She said it as easily as if she were discussing bridge with her lady's club. "I was their human lie detector, and I never failed." she said. "I see people as they really are. It's a gift." she added simply.

"You... see people as they really are?" Kelly asked. Sterling looked at his wife and she smiled, giving him permission to explain.

"Yes, she does. Most of us spend too much time getting in our own way. Trying to analyze things to make them fit our pre-conceived notions of what we think they might be, could be, or should be. Sylvia skips that step." He sipped his beer and continued. "It's an ability she was born with. One that is very valuable to espionage agencies everywhere in the world."

Sterling tensed slightly. "Director Angleton was the CIA's great mastermind of counterespionage during the 70's. He was also a genius, but his paranoia almost destroyed the agency. When he isolated Sylvia and started subjecting her to experiments, I got her out."

Sylvia touched his forearm reassuringly. "It's long in the past sweetheart." She smiled. continuing the tale. "Angleton was resurrecting the old Soviet mind control program, MKULTRA. He thought he could duplicate what I had in other people." She poured Kelly a glass of Chablis. "Their theory was that I must be able to instantaneously analyze tiny involuntary facial movements, muscle shifts and scent changes in a person subliminally. For me, it's just a natural function. I thought everyone could do it. I used to be baffled at how easily others were misled by people with ill intent."

Sylvia buttered a warm piece of her corn bread and bit into it with relish before continuing. "I have no pre-conceived notions or expectations about a person. I really don't know how I do it." Silvia explained. "They couldn't figure out how to re-create it in other people either. Angleton lost patience and decided to try psychotropic drugs and LSD on me. When I refused the drugs, he sequestered me for *"observation"* and began experimenting on me, regardless of my objections. It would have cost me my sanity." she said. "Angleton thought it a small sacrifice."

Her next statement was delivered in a straightforward voice. "That man would have dissected me if he thought it would gain him an advantage."

Sterling put an arm around her. "I was working as a special consultant for the CIA in a high-level D.C. think tank at the time. When I met Sylvia, that was it for me. I was in love with her and I knew I always would be. Then she just disappeared. I knew she'd never willingly do that, so I used my resources to find her. We got her out." Sterling's genial look hardened. "Angleton and I had an understanding about him ever coming after her, or us, again."

"Sterling always finds what he's looking for. Don't you darling?"

"Wasn't that about the time the CIA dropped the MKULTRA project and fired Angleton?" Fletch asked.

Sterling's expression was entirely too self-satisfied when he replied. "Why yes. I believe it was."

Silvia looked at her husband, then back at her guests. "But that's another story we'll save for another day."

"I definitely want to hear it before we leave." Fletch said. ""I have so many questions to ask you."

Kelly stifled a laugh at the understatement.

"I know you do." Sterling acknowledged. "You have my word I'll answer them before you go." He turned to his wife. "Sylvia. How many guests have we asked here in thirty years?"

"Counting our Mr. Grey. Six." she said. "Only six people in thirty years"? Kelly repeated.

Sylvia nodded and smiled. "We collect exceptional individuals, if they're amenable to it. Like anything else exceptional, you're few and far between."

"Exceptional, by our standards, begins here." Sterling touched his heart. "And here." he touched a finger to his temple." Sterling directed his attention to Fletcher.

" You risked your career and your life to follow your instincts and moral code. Don't look so surprised Fletcher." Sterling said. "We make it our business to thoroughly vet anyone we invite here. Sylvia backs it up. She has the final say on the real motives behind your actions." Fletcher lowered his eyes. It was hard for him to take compliments, even if they were just acknowledgements of fact.

"Your commitment to protecting and defending the American people and the woman you obviously love doesn't need a Menschennerin to see it." He continued, pinning Fletch with the truth in his eyes. "You made the hard decisions you needed to make to keep your promises to Kelly and the oath you swore to defend America against all enemies, both foreign and domestic, regardless of the cost to you."

Fletch nodded cautiously. "I suppose I did. Wouldn't anybody?" Sterling gave him a wry grin. "In your line of work, with everything you've seen and done, you'd have to be a true altruist to still believe that. Your tactical skills, integrity, thought processes and self-motivation are just icing on the cake. You're as rare a find as a Statesman is in a politician. We trust Sylvia's talents, but I like to do my research." He added.

Fletcher was quiet, lost for words. It was uncomfortable being stripped down, revealed and evaluated by such a thorough dissection of his true character. Even if it had been a positive evaluation. Like most people, he'd been so busy focusing on what he saw as his faults and failures, he rarely gave himself credit for his strengths and successes.

Sterling nodded at Fletcher, taking his silence as acceptance of his evaluation. He turned his attention to Kelly.

"As for you, Captain Hunter. The airlines have a policy of not resisting hijackers. "Would you define gouging a hijacker's eyes out and crushing his windpipe as not resisting?"

"No." Kelly looked guilty and wondered where this was leading.

"Do you think any of us would be alive now, including people on the ground and in the White House, if you had blindly followed that policy?"

"No." she acknowledged. "I didn't have a choice. At the time, I didn't have the luxury of worrying about it or thinking about them as another human being."

"Why not?" Sylvia asked. "You were willing, ready and in the process of trying to kill him to stop him, weren't you?"

Fletch was ready to jump in and defend Kelly, feeling the questions being directed at her were accusatory and undeserved. Kelly noticed and shook her head, *no*.

"Yes, I was, and I would have if that had been the only way to stop him. As far as I'm concerned, when someone comes into my cockpit with the intention of doing harm to my passengers or my crew, they've decided to commit suicide by Kelly."

Sylvia Sterling considered what Kelly said. Her face revealed nothing but interest. "How do you feel about that now?"

Kelly's brows knitted. "I'm a mess now that I can afford to think of them as someone's son, brother, or husband." She looked down at her hands. "My life will never be the same. I will never be the same." She thought of her young co-pilot. "I'd do it again if I had to." she said. "I just wish…. I wish I'd been quicker."

"Damn right." Sterling agreed. Those are just some of the reasons why you're both here."

In case you haven't noticed," Sylvia added. "You two are more alike than you think you are. Your hearts, your commitment to serving and protecting others, and your integrity are both the same. Your differences in skill sets complement each other. They add to your strengths as a whole." Sylvia looked at her husband. "Just like ours do."

Spencer Sterling lowered his head to a level with Kelly's downcast eyes. His own eyes were filled with compassion and understanding. "Being human and making the hard decisions between survival and a healthy person's drive to treat others with the kindness we'd prefer is hard. It results in a conflict between the spiritual being you are and the animal instinct to do whatever we need to survive. These decisions aren't meant to be easy. They're the catalysts that forge our souls and determine who we are."

"I know why you love and collect Japanese Katanas." Sylvia stated. They remind you of the process life gives us to be the master craftsmen of our spiritual creation" she said. "The forging processes a master swordsmith uses to make a katana from a lump of metal requires months of heating, quenching, pounding out the impurities in the base metal, and folding it thousands of times, over and over again, until it becomes a thing of incredible strength, flexibility, sharpness, beauty, function and reverence." Kelly nodded, surprised at Sylvia's depth of perception. Sylvia smiled and offered Kelly more butter. "You're not a lump of metal dear. You are a Katana."

Kelly blushed. Sylvia couldn't have paid her a better compliment. Like Fletch, she struggled with imposter syndrome.

"It's not a compliment dear. It's an observation." Sylvia sipped her coffee. "I would be doing you a great disservice otherwise."

"Katana's aside," Sterling said. "That's what happened in your cockpit on September 11th." Having a conscience verifies you're a good person who made the hard choices necessary for the survival of yourself and others in your care. Dwelling on it and letting it eat you alive as penance doesn't make you a better person. It cripples you, and those who love you. It prevents you from continuing to be the protector and guardian you are."

I hear what you're saying." Kelly put her fork down.. She'd lost her appetite. "Logic doesn't make a difference." she looked up with haunted eyes. "It's a frightening thing for me when I can't logic my way out of a problem."

"Of course not." Sterling said. "If it was that easy, we wouldn't be losing a dozen of our Veterans a day to PTSD they couldn't live with. "You can believe it in your mind, but until you know it in your heart, you can't heal. You deserve healing." Sterling looked meaningfully at Fletcher. "As a professional warrior, I'm sure you understand this better than most" Fletcher nodded. "All the time." he said.

"Are we good?" he asked Kelly." She nodded. "I think Sylvia's rubbing off on you."

"I can only hope so." Sterling said, with a grin of his own. He rubbed his hands together in anticipation. "Sylvia, my love, can you rustle up some hot toddies or some of your special spiced Mexican hot chocolate for us? It's getting a little chilly out here. I'm enjoying everything about this day too much to go inside." he said. "I'll have a nice fire going in the fire pit for us by the time you get back," he said. "Do you need any help in there?"

"Heavens no Spencer. The Kitchen's my domain. Remember what happened when you tried to bake me a birthday cake." She cautioned.

Sylvia bent down to Kelly and Fletch. "He's a genius in everything else he touches." she said. "My birthday cake came out looking beautiful on the outside, but he dropped it when he tried to pick it up. It weighed thirty pounds, hard as a rock, and it shattered into a dozen pieces when it hit the floor." Sylvia stood up and headed for the kitchen. "I think you did that on purpose Sylvan, just to let me have one thing I'm better at than you." She called over her shoulder.

"She still has me tripping over my own feet like a lovesick teenager." Sterling grinned. "That's my excuse and I'm sticking with it. Would you rather go inside?" he asked.

Kelly and Fletch shook their heads "no" in unison. Fletch looked at Kelly. "We rarely get to enjoy wood smoke and campfires in such beautiful surroundings and in such good company." he said. "We're fine right here."

Sterling looked pleased and nodded. "I apologize if it seemed like I was grilling you Kelly. I wasn't. Sylvia picked up on your struggles with the things you had to do to keep us all alive on 9/11. I wanted to make sure you knew you made the right choices, and you did the right things. And no, Kelly." he assured her. "You are not a monster or a budding serial killer." Sterling laughed softly as he said this. "I say this because I've walked a mile in your shoes, as have most good soldiers like Fletcher, and they suffer for it."

Sylvia came down the stairs with a tray of copper mugs filled with hot chocolate, and the toddies Sterling requested. The heady scent of spices, lemon and a splash of rum followed her as she set the tray down. She handed Kelly a mug of the Mexican Chocolate. "Careful, it's hot." she warned, sitting down next to Kelly with a blanket and a mug of her own.

Sylvia continued her evaluation of Kelly. "Aside from your obvious skills flying anything with wings or rotors, and your Martial Arts. You excel in things that interest you, and you work hard to see it successfully completed." Sylvia continued. "You're what we call a Start -Do-Complete person. As a leader, you genuinely value and care about others. You want to see them excel. People notice this, and instinctively trust and choose to follow you."

Kelly nodded. She'd never thought of herself quite like that, but it did make sense. She worked hard and rose to challenges by doggedly pursuing them through to their conclusions. "I make mistakes like everyone else Sylvia." she said. "I just try to excel at recovery."

Sterling nodded his approval. "I think you broke the code on that."

Kelly shrugged and nodded. "That's part of the briefing I give to all my new co-pilots before flying together for the first time."

"Those are a few of the reasons why we invited both of you here, and why we're trusting you with some of our little secrets. It gets lonely at the top." He chuckled.

Kelly was beginning to feel like they were being evaluated for a job interview.

Even if the Sterlings were doing it in the most personable and delightful ways.

"The..ah…technology?" Fletch began. He didn't know where to start. "The appearance of food and firewood out of nowhere? The apparent barrier to wind, rain, and, I suspect, flying obstacles like birds and bullets? The barrier still lets in the fragrances of the desert and automatically allows us to pass through it?"

"What about the helicopter?" Kelly asked. "The noise and vibration stopped. The rotor blades slowed but kept turning. The engine seemed to have quit as soon as we neared your ranch? At least, I don't think the engine was running." Kelly said uncertainly. "The sound and vibration stopped in a seamless transition." She looked at Fletch.

"I think you'd better answer Fletch's questions first. They've been driving him nuts. Kelly's forehead wrinkled. "I'm beginning to think I'm nuts for even asking a question like that." She muttered under her breath.

Sterling's chuckle led to a full-blown belly laugh. It escalated until tears trickled out of the corners of his eyes. Sylvia's unsuccessful attempts to stop him with half-hearted taps on his arm and protestations of "Sterling. Stop that and just tell them." only landed her in a similar giggle fit.

"I'm sorry." Sylvia gasped. "Sterling likes to put on a performance for his friends. It's his guilty pleasure." She said, dabbing at her own tears with a napkin.

"It's not exactly matter transmission." Sylvia remarked. "Not yet. We're working on that too." she said. "We do bend light waves around objects to make things appear to be invisible. We use sound frequencies and electro-magnetic energy to move and levitate things."

"Some people refer to it as anti-gravity." Sterling added." It's a little simplistic, but the term applies it all 3 dimensions, including the ability to control instant G-force acceleration to speeds where the human body would otherwise be crushed."

Sterling took a sip of his toddy and sighed with pleasure. "You two ok?" he asked, noticing their wide-eyed silence. Kelly blinked and looked at Fletcher. "We're fine. Just riveted, and trying to wrap our minds around all this." Fletcher nodded. "Please, don't stop now. This is incredible. Wonderful." He added. "Don't leave us hanging."

The Sterlings looked pleased. Particularly Sylvan. Kelly got the impression he rarely had the opportunity to share his passions and accomplishments with an equally enthusiastic audience. He grinned and nodded at Sylvia to continue.

"Both the alcove and the outdoor firewood alcove have quick and seamless moveable surfaces with a holographic feature that makes them appear to be empty until we cloak or uncloak the food. Simple really." Sylvia assured them. "The Algorithms predict and prepare your favorite habitual choices in food in minutes. The same with the firewood. Vibrational particle manipulation with the rain and object barrier as well." Fletch and Kelly were mesmerized. Their minds tying to process everything Sylvia was telling them.

"As to the soundless levitation, in answer to your questions, Kelly. We're working on electro-magnetism, gravitational manipulation, and many of those sciences. As you observed, we've been quite successful. The continuing rotation of the rotor blades are just for show, to disguise the technology from people we don't want to attract the interest of. As were the vibrations."

"Developing and applying the technology is the easy fun part for us." Sterling said.

"Then there's the not-so-fun dangerous down-side of our successes." He frowned. "We're under constant surveillance by many governments, including our own. Industrial espionage by corporations large and small, legal and illegal, is just a fact of life for us. We use many of the technologies we're developing to shield and protect ourselves."

Sterling and Sylvia exchanged a look with each other before he continued. "If either of you have any doubts or concerns about being willing and able to keep what I'm going to tell you in the strictest confidentiality, now is the time to tell us. We'll discuss it no further." Sterling folded his arms and waited.

Fletcher and Kelly exchanged concerned glances. "Is anything you're going to tell us illegal, unethical, Unconstitutional or harmful to the American people? Fletch asked. "For that matter," Kelly added. "Is it harmful or going to be used to enslave or harm the people of the world in general?" She asked. "You're not going to go all Dr. Strangelove, or James Bond super-villain on us are you?

"If you are," Fletcher said, "you might as well call your silent helicopter and take us home right now. I think I speak for both of us." Kelly nodded.

Sterling raised his hands as if to ward off something unthinkable. "No! No. Absolutely not." He protested. "In fact. Quite the opposite." Sylvia added. "This is about preventing industrial espionage, our personal safety and keeping our technologies out of the hands of entities who would use them for exactly the purposes you're concerned about. If you still have misgivings, of course you're free to go at any time."

"We take that, your well-being and your trust very seriously." Kelly said. "What do you think Fletch?" He was quiet for a long time before answering. "Risk-rewards considered," he said. "Kelly and I are already up to our ears in sworn secrecy and a lie about our hijacking. I say, we have nothing to lose by keeping our confidences to you." Kelly nodded in agreement. "I'm in." Sterling looked relieved. Sylvia let out the breath she'd been holding.

"Good to hear, and done." Sterling said. "I rarely meet people whose word is as good as their bond. If you're willing, I'll continue. These measures protect you as well as us."

A holographic screen appeared above the sandstone table, showing a 3-dimensional full color image of the Sterling Ranch restricted area. "If you look for the Sterling Ranch restricted area on Google Earth satellite imagery, what you'll see there isn't what you see here. We have an alter ego display letting the satellites and other monitoring devices see what we want them to see, and hear what we want them to hear."

"Concentrated directional sound frequencies above and below the human hearing range fill would-be trespassers with feelings of dread, fear and panic…the closer they get, the more intense the effects become. Then headaches, racing thoughts and the inability to think. We've never had anyone get closer to the boundaries of Sterling Ranch than a quarter mile."

"We're actually a little disappointed in that." Sylvia said. "Remember the flash gadget memory eraser in the Men in Black? We've been wanting to test ours out, but considering what was done to me, we still have some ethical concerns about using it." She laughed.

"On a serious note." Sterling said. "Sylvia and I took a chance when we invited you here. I don't know if we had a right to do that." he said.

"Why not. What do you mean?" Fletcher asked. His face mirrored the concern on Kelly's."

"Did you tell anyone anything other than the story you two were gifted an all-expense paid vacation to a private location by a grateful anonymous donor?"

Kelly and Fletch looked at each other. "No. Why?"

"Because you would be tracked, hounded, and threatened by people, governments, and corporations if they thought you'd come here or had this kind of a connection with us. I should have told you first, but we thought you had enough worries and stresses to deal with at the time. I can assure you that no-one suspects you're here. We're constantly monitoring all communications with a basic form of artificial intelligence keyed exactly for this purpose."

"We're currently mastering the simple stuff." Sylvia said. "Most governments around the world already have a start on it. They're in a no-holds-barred race to get them first. Whether they get these technologies through their own research and development or steal it from us, or each other. They have no qualms about killing for it."

"Fortunately, none of them are as close to mastering and achieving control of these technologies as we are." Sterling added. "Bending light, vibrational sound frequencies above and below the range of human hearing that can move things and elicit any emotions we choose for people within range. Emotions including euphoria and feelings of deep dread and fear."

Kelly and Fletch looked at each other, mirroring their conflicting expressions of awe and dread. Sylvia didn't miss a beat validating their concerns.

"We agree with you completely. They're simultaneously wonderful technologies, full of hope for mankind, and they're absolutely terrifying technologies if they fall into the hands of those who will use them to control the minds and the free will of whole populations of people, on both a national and an international scale."

"Real teleportation is closer than we think." Sterling continued, riding a wave of enthusiasm for the science. "Time control? Not so much. Unintended consequences and all that." Sterling said. "Mother nature doesn't seem to like me messing with her molecules." he continued.

"Our goal here at Sterling Ranch and in the very close cadre' of scientists and operatives we have, is to stay two steps ahead of the technological advances governments around the world are making to remain competitive in the arms race." Sylvan shook his head. "It's a catch 22, and a moral dilemma." Sterling was staring at something in a not-so-distant future only he could see. "If we don't do it, the other guy will. That, and the fact that wars are very profitable for the worldwide military Industrial complex." he took a sip of water, waiting for his revelations t sink in.

"Who, exactly, is behind all of the obfuscation and mis-direction anyway?' Kelly asked. "Is it even possible to prevent abuses of technology?"

Seeing the data-overwhelm looks on Kelly and Fletcher's faces, Sylvia stepped in.

"Simply put" she said. "It's just the same old Feudal System mentality the self-defined elite have always thought they're entitled to. There's really nothing new about their self-proclaimed New World Order. They've never really stopped trying to control the free world." She said." America is a major thorn in their sides. The American people, as a whole and as individuals, like being rewarded for our own hard work, innovation and independence. We're a stubborn and self-sufficient lot." she said. "Unfortunately, some who've known nothing else are all too willing to sell their freedoms for a handout." A cloud passed over Sylvia's bright face. She shook it off. "Enough of that." She said.

Sylvia put a hand on Sterling's shoulder saying. "Considering what Kelly and Fletcher have been through, I think we can move on to enjoying ourselves and perhaps giving Kelly and Fletcher a chance to play with some of your toys in the next few days." She smiled at Fletch and Kelly. "Of course, only if you'd like to. Don't let us overwhelm you darlings." Sylvia said. "It's such a rare treat for us to have guests like you to share our enthusiasm with." She snuggled closer to Sterling. "We refused to sign the adult contract a long time ago." A slight dimple formed in her cheek when she smiled. "We were far too serious when we were children, so we're having our first childhood now." She looked at her husband, who smiled back at her in agreement.

"She's right you know." He said, squeezing her hand. "The couple closed their eyes, immersed in their enjoyment of each other and their moment. They looked like they were counting their blessings.

Not the least of which, Fletch thought, *were each other.* Calm and contentment radiated off the older couple. Filling the room and enfolding Kelly and Fletch in a sense of safety and well-being. Putting the world and its fleeting struggles and grievances in perspective.

Sylvan opened his eyes. He gave Sylvia's hand a gentle squeeze and said, "The world has changed on a daily-basis. It's facing major challenges in the foreseeable future. Great difficulties also create great opportunities. The events of September 11th this year were just the tip of the iceberg. The parties who orchestrated this go far beyond the puppets of Al Qaeda.

"We do what we can." Sylvia added. We've had far more successes than you'd think. You'll never hear of them, or us, on the news media. Nor should you, if we're doing our job right."

She turned her clear guileless eyes on Kelly and Fletcher. Sylvia smiled and leaned toward them. "Every generation throughout history has had one crisis or another to deal with." she said. "We generally come out the better for it, developing solutions. Hopefully, learning from our mistakes. When the world changes overnight, like it did on 9/11, it's not always for the worse." She said, readjusting the blanket on her lap. "The native Americans knew this. They call magic, a change in perception.

Think of the mass transformative change that happened overnight between the horror of September 11th and the self-sacrifice, kinship, kindness, and support strangers showed each other on September 12th.

No one cared whether you were, black, white, gay, straight, or what political party you belonged to. On 9/12. We looked in each other's eyes and saw each other's hearts, each other's pain. On that day we were all American brothers and sisters, committed to each other's safety, our country and to the promise we would never let this happen again." Sylvia sighed. "There are so many unsung heroes every day, that we never hear about."

She moved from Sterling to take a seat between Kelly and Fletcher, putting her hands on theirs. It felt comfortable and soothing. "The truth is, there is far more beauty in this world than there is ugliness. There are far more good people in this world doing far more good things for each other than bad. Far more tiny daily miracles, unsung heroes and small acts of kindness that change someone's world for the better. They're so common we don't recognize them as the miracles they are, or our guardian angels as anything more than strangers gifting us with a small kindness when we need it most."

Sylvia looked at Fletcher, then Kelly with that clear innocent gaze she had, an ancient wisdom filled with child-like wonder shining through. "You were never meant to bear the weight of the world alone. None of us are. It's ok to let it go. Let others help you and find their own way to shine."

"This is why we do what we do. These are the people we're fighting for." Sterling added. "That said, if we're not having a grand adventure rising to these challenges, we're not doing it right. Life is meant to be a banquet, not a burden."

Fletch grinned. "I like the way you think Sterling." Kelly smiled and raised her hot chocolate in agreement. "I second that."

Pouring herself a cup of coffee from the French press, Sylvia tilted her head and gave her husband a questioning look. Sterling smiled and nodded.

"Sterling and I are committed to not leaving this life with any regrets." Sylvia said. Her smile became surprisingly predatory. "You could say, we *disincentivize* corrupt bad actors manipulating events like 9/11 for profit and power. We make it profitable, and in their own best interest, for them to do the right thing."

She paused before saying. "You both seem to live by that mission statement as well." She stirred a teaspoon of honey into her coffee. "Take a month or so to consider our offer before deciding." She said, "Sterling and I are hoping you two might consider doing some free-lance work for us on occasion, as part of our team and our family."